HOUSE OF DREAMS

In the small Cornish village of Tregorran, Demelza struggles to keep the family house intact and care for her young brothers and sister after the deaths of her parents. Knowing that she is losing the battle, she agrees to take in a paying guest: handsome Lucas Fairfield. But the growing attraction between the two seems doomed from the start. With Lucas obliged to return to his ancestral manor in Hampshire, and Demelza devoted to caring for her siblings and own familial home in Tregorran, can they ever find happiness together?

FENELLA J. MILLER

◆

HOUSE OF DREAMS

Complete and Unabridged

LINFORD
Leicester

First published in Great Britain in 2013

First Linford Edition
published 2014

A catalogue record for this book is available
from the British Library.

ISBN 978–1–4448–2008–9

1

The window blew open, smashing back against the wall. Demelza shot up in bed. The curtains were horizontal, the rain cascading onto the worn boards. Tumbling out from beneath the covers, she dashed across and slammed the window shut.

Thunder growled and the night air was rent by forks of lightning. In the glow from this she saw the bobbing lanterns of a ship on the edge of the bay. The vessel was in trouble, caught up in mountainous waves and in danger of being smashed against the rocks. She sent up a fervent prayer that the lives of those on board would be spared and by some miracle the ship would not sink. She shivered. There had been more than one wreck off Tregorran village in her lifetime — she prayed tonight there would not be another.

The curtains were sodden and she was standing in a puddle. She'd better get dressed before her nightgown was as wet as the floor. It would be dawn soon; hardly worth going back to bed as she was wide awake.

Whilst the storm continued to rage, the rain would be pouring in through the holes in the roof. The buckets must need emptying. After dressing by a single flickering candle, she hung her damp nightdress over the end of the bed and hurried out. Serena didn't like storms, but her brothers, Tom and Jack, rarely woke.

Demelza pushed open the door to her little sister's room. On this side of the house the rain beat with less force. She listened. Good — her sister was sleeping. She must complete the domestic tasks before full light because Buttercup would need milking then. Serena, at ten years old, was quite capable of dressing the boys and taking care of them for a short while.

Twenty minutes later the buckets

were empty and the storm had passed. Today was going to be another warm summer's day. As always, Demelza had left the bread to rise before she retired the night before, so it wouldn't take long to shape to dough and put it in the bread oven. She raked the kitchen fire and pushed kindling into the glowing embers. She filled the kettle and hung it from the trivet to heat.

Today Buttercup produced a full pail of foaming, creamy milk. 'What a good girl. Now you can feed your calf; I shan't need any more until tomorrow.' Carefully carrying the milk into the dairy, she placed it on the slate shelf and covered it with a wet cloth. Five minutes later the bellowing calf was reunited with his mother and Demelza was heading inside.

The children wouldn't be awake for an hour or two, which gave her plenty of time to escape to the beach that ran below the cliffs upon which Tregorran House was built. Her boots left wet imprints on the grass as she ran to the path which threaded down the cliff. She could hear the waves banging; although the storm had passed, the sea was still rough. Thick gorse bushes grew on either side, obscuring her view of the beach as she descended.

Leaving her boots at the bottom of the path, she stepped barefoot onto the rain-washed sand. She glanced at the sky. The seagulls were calling overhead; even the waves couldn't drown their raucous cries. She had come fearing she might find flotsam and jetsam littering the coastline, but the sand was pristine. Thank God! No ships had foundered on the rocks last night.

If she was lucky she would be able to collect a crab or two and pick mussels from the rocks. Without this free bounty she and the children would be on short commons indeed. The tide would be turning soon; she must hurry or she would be trapped by the waves.

The best place to find shellfish was in the rock pools. The white-capped waves didn't deter her. As she bent to move the seaweed aside, her eye was caught by something just ahead. She straightened. She wasn't alone. A gentleman was crouching over the very pool she was heading for.

Her bucket dropped with a clatter. Oh dear! She was hardly dressed for meeting company. The man, startled by the noise, stumbled backwards and fell seat-first into the shallow pool.

'I beg your pardon, sir. I didn't mean to scare you . . . '

Periwinkle blue eyes stared at her; despite their pretty colour they were not friendly. 'Are you going to stand there gawping, girl, or assist me to escape from this wretched water?'

Demelza bristled. He took her for a village maid but that gave him no right to be uncivil. 'Are you injured?'

'Of course not. Now, are you going to help me or not?'

She smiled demurely and dipped in a mock curtsy. 'Not. I've better things to do with my time, sir, than pull an unpleasant gentleman from his backside. I bid you good morning.'

'Come back here, you baggage. Devil take it!' Splashing and further cursing followed her departure.

Recovering her pail, she skipped nimbly in the opposite direction, her ears burning at his reply to her impertinence. She would return this evening when the beach was empty. She paused halfway up the steep cliff path and looked back. The man was upright and balancing on one leg to empty water from a boot. Even from this distance she could see he was a prodigious height, his shoulders broad and his fair hair worn long so that it curled on his collar.

His manners were poor but she couldn't fault his appearance. When she walked down to the village later she would discover who he was. In Tregorran a stranger was noted immediately. After all, had she not heard the very same day about the arrival of the rough men from Polperro? Mrs Newlyn would be able to tell her who he was and what he was doing in Cornwall. He obviously wasn't a customs man; judging from his apparel he was a man of means. She couldn't remember the last time such a person had come to this neighbourhood.

Maybe she wouldn't go herself but send Serena. For some reason, she wasn't eager to renew her acquaintance with the formidable stranger she'd inadvertently tipped into the sea.

* * *

Lucas watched her go. His mouth curved. Who was that adorable Cornish maid? From the moment he'd seen her glaring down at him, he'd been intrigued. Those flashing green eyes and lustrous black locks were not the only things that attracted him. She was both spirited and intelligent. In fact, she was everything he'd ever wanted in a young lady. She was obviously gently bred. She must come from the dilapidated manor house he'd spied on the hilltop outside the village.

He would return and quiz his landlady for information. For the first time in many months his step was light. Could this chance encounter be the beginning of his recovery?

He squelched into the inn yard. 'Mrs Newlyn, I wish to speak to you.'

His landlady hurried out, her face red from baking. 'Yes, sir, what can I do for you?' Her smile slipped. 'My word! You're a mite wet!'

'A young woman tipped me into a rock pool. I believe she comes from the big house on the cliff. Can you tell me anything about her?'

'That will be Demelza Tregorran. This village is named after her family — it's a right shame she's likely to lose her home.' The woman rubbed her floury hands across her eyes. 'Since poor Mr Tregorran went to meet his maker a year past, things have gone from bad to worse. That little family will not survive another winter the way things are, you mark my words.'

'There is no relative who can step in and assist?'

'There's an uncle in London, but they don't want to move to a dirty old city. The Tregorrans are fighters. She'll keep them here as long as she can. What they needs is a miracle.'

'I see. If you will excuse me, Mrs Newlyn, I must change my garments.'

He ducked his head as he walked in to avoid the beams and bounded up the narrow stairs to his chamber. By the time he was dry he knew exactly what he would do. He must speak to his landlady forthwith.

★ ★ ★

The house was quiet; the children must still be asleep. Demelza set the table and checked the water was almost boiling before taking a basket and hurrying to the hen house to collect eggs for breakfast. She went into the

9

kitchen garden to gather a few handfuls of strawberries.

This area was protected from sea breezes by a high stone wall. She sighed. It used to be more productive, but since Pa died there had been no one to till the soil apart from her. She shouldn't complain. Many families were on the brink of destitution — although those that were involved in smuggling were slightly better off. Even the men who were part of the small fishing fleet no longer garnered an adequate income from their work. Would the impoverished be persuaded to join the incomers? The revenue men would never turn a blind eye to a group not led by locals.

She pushed the worrying thoughts aside. Her annuity was just enough to keep body and soul together; she needn't resort to illegal pastimes to supplement her income. She returned to the kitchen to discover Tom, Jack and Serena sitting at the table eagerly awaiting their breakfast.

'Good morning, children. You must be starving. I know I am.'

Demelza placed a dish of coddled eggs and several slices of warm bread dripping with butter next to each child. She devoured her breakfast as eagerly as they. Meeting the irascible man on the beach had sharpened her appetite. 'Would you like some honey to finish up your bread, Serena?'

Her sister grinned, unable to speak because her mouth was too full. Tom and Jack bounced up and down to attract her attention. 'We want some too, please, Melza.'

'I'm going into the village. Do you want to come with me?'

'No thank you, Melza. Serena's taking us to the beach to build a sandcastle,' Tom said.

'Not this morning, sweetheart; the tide's coming in. You'll have to wait until tomorrow. I know all three of you swim like little eels but it's not safe. It's still rough after the storm last night.' She smiled. 'I'm surprised you slept through it. I've just got to check the buckets and tidy myself before I go. Behave whilst I'm away; I shan't be long.'

Demelza left Serena in charge of the dirty dishes. Taking a jug of hot water, she went upstairs to her chamber to remove any remaining sand from her bare legs. She wanted to look her best when she went to the village.

A quarter of an hour later she was ready. Today she scooped her hair up and secured it with pins. Hopefully her straw bonnet would keep it in place, as her locks had a maddening tendency to tumble down her back. She viewed her image in the long glass her mother had brought with her when she'd married Pa all those years ago. Her gown was old but clean, and a pretty shade of pink. It hugged her waist and fitted snugly over her bosom. She frowned and tugged at the neckline. Did it reveal rather too much of her curves? Well it was too late to repine; she had nothing else and there was no one in Tregorran she wanted to impress.

All her garments were old and in need of replacing, but what little money there was for clothing she spent on the children. They were growing like weeds, especially Serena. Ma had taught her to sew, and without this skill they would likely look like ragamuffins. When her mother had succumbed to a congestion of the lungs three winters ago, Pa never recovered. He had given up on life and slowly faded away. He'd followed Ma into the damp ground last winter, unable to continue without his soul mate. Demelza wondered if she herself would someday meet a man whom she couldn't live without.

She laughed at her nonsense. Pa had been of a whimsical nature, unlike Ma, who had been made of sterner stuff. Tregorrans had always lived in this huge, draughty house and she was determined to keep the family together until the boys were full-grown and could take over the small estate. Until then she would manage alone. If she could find a little extra money each month it would be possible to employ journey-men to cultivate the neglected fields. The income generated from this would produce enough to repair her home. Tregorran House had been self-sufficient before Ma died — it could be made to pay its way again.

Demelza collected her basket and set out. The children were old enough to be left for an hour or two without supervision. She skipped sideways to avoid two cats hissing and spitting in the yard. They abandoned their fight when they saw her. 'Sorry, I've nothing for you. Perhaps tonight I'll have some scraps.'

When their terrier, Patch, had died a few months ago, she had promised the children a puppy for their name day. She must begin her search for a suitable animal. Maybe someone in the village would have a dog she could take. Fortunately the cats fed themselves most of the time and appeared content with the few scraps she sometimes gave them. The chickens were obliged to do the same. She was sure if she could afford extra grain they would lay eggs more frequently.

Her eyes filled. She didn't mind for herself, but the children had lost so much. They were orphans, relying on her for everything, and she was slowly losing the battle to provide for them. They were unlikely to survive another winter and she would have to agree to move to London.

After drying her eyes on her sleeve, she sniffed inelegantly. On such a glorious summer's day, how could she be shedding tears over something that might never happen? The half mile to the village was downhill but was always hard work coming back with a laden basket. She stopped and gazed at the huddle of stone houses crouching around the natural harbour.

Tregorran had once been a happy place where folk helped each other out and no one was allowed to starve when things were tough. Things were different recently. She was aware of malevolence in the stares of some of the unemployed villagers. They must blame her for not helping them as her parents had once done.

She was greeted by a few villagers but didn't stop to gossip. She headed straight for the tavern. Inside the Green Man the air was smoky and dark and the appetising smell of meat pasties wafted from the kitchen.

Mrs Newlyn bustled out from the back, wiping her hands on her apron. 'Demelza, my lovely, come to buy your lunch, have you? Nasty old storm last night, weren't there?'

'I hope no boats were lost. I saw a ship heading for the rocks in our bay but it appears to have sailed safely by.'

Mrs Newlyn glanced over her shoulder before answering, as if afraid someone might be eavesdropping. 'Thank the good Lord for that. None of our boys were out in the storm. I reckon I know why you're here, my dear.'

Demelza knew her cheeks were pink.

'Is that man staying here, Mrs Newlyn?'

'The gent from London, you mean? Fine young man. He came back in a right old mood with his breeches wet and his boots full of water. Said something about a Cornish maid tipping him into a rock pool. I reckoned you'd be down here asking.'

'I didn't do any such thing. I dropped my bucket and the noise startled him. I can't be blamed if the man can't keep on his feet . . . '

A rich chuckle coming from the depths of a wooden settle made her jump. She spun to see the very man she'd come to enquire about, watching her with amusement. She hadn't noticed him in the gloom.

'We haven't been introduced.' He uncurled and stood looming over her. He bowed politely. 'Lucas Fairfield, at your service.'

Mrs Newlyn looked as flustered as Demelza. 'This is Miss Demelza Tregorran. Lives up the big house with her brothers and sister like I told you.'

'I'm pleased to meet you, Mr Fairfield. I'm glad to see you suffered no permanent damage from your soaking.' His eyes flashed a warning and she wished she hadn't mentioned the incident.

The landlady shifted uncomfortably. 'I were going to come and see you today, my lovely. Mr Fairfield is looking for more comfortable lodgings and I reckon you've got plenty of room up at that old house of yours.'

Demelza was about to refuse outright, as the last person she wanted sharing her home was this unsettling person, but he forestalled her.

'We got off to an unfortunate start, Miss Tregorran. May I be the first to apologise for using strong language in your presence?'

She had no choice. 'And I beg your pardon for being the unwitting cause of your unfortunate experience.'

'Mr Fairfield, Demelza, why don't you sit on the bench outside? I'll bring out refreshments and you can discuss terms.' Mrs Newlyn vanished into the kitchens and he smiled in a most disconcerting way.

'An excellent idea. I'm constantly banging my head on these beams. After you, Miss Tregorran.' He gestured towards the door and somehow she was in the sunshine with a man who made her feel decidedly uncomfortable.

'I don't think I can offer you accommodation, sir. I live alone with my siblings. Even here folk would gossip.'

He frowned. 'Do you have no staff?'

'None at all. That's why — '

He rudely interrupted. 'Then the matter is solved. I shall employ staff for you: a cook, a parlour maid, and another girl should be enough for indoors. A gardener, a stable boy and two outside men to work in the fields should do for a start.'

How dare he presume to order her life like this? 'You shall do no such thing, Mr Fairfield. If — and I have not yet decided on the matter — you do

19

become my lodger, it will be on my terms, and any staff involved shall be employed by me.' She glared at him, daring him to contradict. His mouth curved and he raised a hand as if to calm her down. 'Anyway, I'm sure you're aware staff don't count when it comes to a lady's reputation. I need a female companion.'

'I see. Do you know any such person in the neighbourhood?'

'As it happens, I do. The rector has his sister staying. She would be ideal if I could persuade her to come.' Good heavens! What was she thinking of? She didn't want this man living with her; he was far too dictatorial for her taste.

'Then you must go and speak to her at once. All that remains is for us to agree a price.' He named a sum so large Demelza was temporarily speechless.

'That's far too much. Half that amount will be sufficient.'

'As you wish.' He dipped into his topcoat and produced a bag which clinked enticingly. 'This should be ample for you to arrange things as I wish.' He tossed the bag in her direction and she had no option but to catch it. 'I shall require a bedchamber, a dressing room and private parlour.' He raised an eyebrow as if expecting her to say he couldn't have these things.

'Of course, sir. Do you have a manservant with you, or a groom?'

'No, I'm travelling alone. I shall remain here tonight, but expect me first thing tomorrow morning. I assume your stables are habitable. My gelding requires decent accommodation.'

'He will have to share the barn with the house cow and her calf, but the roof is sound and we have plenty of straw and hay at the moment.' The church clock struck the hour. If she was to see Mrs Smith before she returned she mustn't dawdle. 'I shall bid you good day, Mr Fairfield. I can assure you everything will be in order by tomorrow morning.'

She walked away, regretting her agreement with every step she took, but the reassuring weight of the money bag told her she had made the right decision. She was a woman of substance now; she could make life more comfortable for the children and start bringing the dilapidated house back to life.

2

Demelza hesitated at the gate to the rectory. If she went to speak to Mrs Smith, then she wouldn't have time to make the purchases she needed and still be back within the hour. No, she wouldn't allow her life to be dictated by a man she had only just met; she would do her shopping and come back to the village in the afternoon.

As she was turning away, someone called, 'Miss Tregorran, I was coming to see you. How fortuitous you should be outside the gate at this very moment.' A tall, thin lady of indeterminate years hurried towards her.

'Mrs Smith, how strange. I was coming to see *you* later. I have a few things to buy but if you would care to walk with me, I should be delighted to have you come back for a visit afterwards.'

'Then I shall do exactly that. What was it you wish to see me about, my dear?'

Demelza explained the situation and her companion listened with an open mouth. 'It's divine intervention, my dear. I prayed for deliverance from the never-ending complaints of my sister-in-law, and here you are offering me sanctuary. I shall come this afternoon and I do not require paying. Indeed, I can give you a small amount towards the housekeeping in return for my keep.'

Demelza was about to refuse this offer but realised Mrs Smith might need to contribute so she no longer felt a burden. 'I can't believe we never thought of this solution before. You're already a firm favourite with the children. I believe with two of us working we can bring the vegetable garden back to full production.'

'I do hope so,' Mrs Smith replied. 'I'm willing to do anything I can to assist.'

'Before you dash away, can you tell me anything about my future house-guest?'

'According to my brother he's a wealthy man recovering from some family disaster. Mr Fairfield fancies himself as an amateur artist and intends to spend the summer dabbling in such activities before resuming his duties elsewhere.'

Demelza snorted inelegantly. 'An artist? He's not built for such pastimes, Mrs Smith.'

'Come now, my dear, you must call me by my given name. In future, I shall be Martha and you Demelza.' Not staying to hear any argument on this point, Martha hurried off to the rectory to pack her belongings.

With her basket full, Demelza began the strenuous walk uphill to her home. She transferred her burden to the other arm and paused for a moment to gaze out across the sea. Divine intervention indeed! This morning she had been in despair. Now everything was different.

When she returned, the children had completed their morning tasks and were about to go out to play. 'I'm glad I found you here. I've exciting news.' When she had finished her explanation, the boys were dancing around in excitement.

'Melza, we like Mrs Smith, don't we, Jack? She tells us stories and likes to play hunt-the-thimble.' Tom jumped up and down, his dark hair flopping over his eyes.

'Does Mr Fairfield have a big horse? Will he let us ride it?'

'He does indeed, Jack, but I'm certain he will not allow you anywhere near it. I must return to the village and find the staff Mr Fairfield insists I employ.'

Serena waited until her brothers had run off across the springy grass before commenting. 'Is Mr Fairfield handsome, Melza? Is he very rich? What's he doing in Tregorran anyway?'

'Yes to the first two questions, and I'm not sure about the last. I have not yet come up with a satisfactory answer. I met him early this morning rummaging through a rock pool. Mrs Smith believes him to be an artist but I think he might be a botanist or something of that ilk.'

Tom and Jack were shouting and waving for Serena to join them.

'Hurry, sweetheart, the boys are waiting. It will have to be bread and cheese at midday as I must get a room ready for Mrs Smith when I get back.'

* * *

Demelza all but ran down to the village. When she had been in Tregorran earlier, Mrs Newlyn had mentioned that Jethro and Molly Trewith couldn't afford the rent on their tiny cottage. Jethro had injured his leg in an accident recently and was now lame and could no longer go out to sea to earn his living. She would go and see them and offer employment and a roof over their heads. There was a cottage behind her house which had once been used for staff. This dwelling had not been occupied for a while, but with a little attention could soon be warm and snug again. There were a couple of local girls she knew of who would also be glad to work for her. Jethro would have to find the outside men.

She tied the ribbons of her bonnet more securely and set off down the High Street. It took her more than a quarter of an hour to climb the winding path that led up to the cottage where Jethro and Molly were living. She knocked and was relieved to hear footsteps inside.

'Well, my lovely, what a pleasure to see you this fine day. Won't you come in? Molly's in the garden; you come along through.'

'Good morning, Jethro. You look well. Such a beautiful day; I do hope the weather is set fair for the next week or so.'

He stared gloomily at the cloudless

sky. 'Don't reckon it'll be staying fine for long, miss.'

Demelza followed him as he limped through the single room that served as both kitchen and parlour and into the back where Molly was pegging out washing. Despite his infirmity, Jethro was remarkably fit for his years. Although not large in stature, he more than made up for it in girth. Greetings over, she explained why she had come and they were overjoyed to be offered a lifeline.

'Can you start immediately? Mr Fairfield is most insistent that staff be employed. He's not used to doing for himself.'

'We'll be there later today, Miss Tregorran. As soon as these here clothes are dry we can gather our things together. We don't have much to carry.' Molly was as tiny as her husband was round; she was a happy soul and would make a cheerful addition to the household.

'Another thing,' Demelza added. 'I don't suppose you know of anyone who has a pony and cart or something similar for sale?'

Jethro's rosy cheeks swelled and he chuckled. 'As a matter of fact I do. Young Johnny Pencarrow came back from Truro with a fancy gig and a smart horse. I don't reckon he's sold that old mare of his yet.'

'If she's old, will she be able to work for me?'

'Bless you, my lovely, old Bessie's got a good few more years in her. She'll do you a treat. I'll come with you now. Young Johnny's not working at the moment. Tide's wrong, if you know what I mean.'

Demelza knew exactly what he was referring to. Young Johnny, thus called to distinguish him from his father who was Old Johnny, was the leader of the local smugglers' gang.

★ ★ ★

By noon she was the proud possessor of a decent-sized trap, an amiable dun-coloured mare and two house maids,

Betty and Josie. Her four new employees and their meagre possessions were sitting in the back of the cart. This time she was returning with one of the famous meat pies from The Green Man. Such luxury to be able to eat a meal she hadn't made from scratch herself. Three barley twists were safely in her reticule for the children.

On their arrival they were greeted by screams of delight. 'We've been waiting ages, Melza. Is the horse and trap ours?' Tom pushed his brother aside in his eagerness to be the first to greet the new arrivals.

'Tom, this is Bessie. See how pleased she is to be here. She's flicking her ears back and forth. Come and greet Jethro and Molly, who will be working here and will be living in the cottage.' She scrambled down and hugged her brothers. 'This is Josie and her sister Betty. They will be living in the attic and helping with the inside tasks.'

Serena was delegated to unlock the cottage and show Molly and Jethro around. Her sister trotted back a short while later with a list of what was needed. Before long, sufficient bedding and bits of furniture had been discovered and transferred to the cottage. Tonight they were all to eat together, but in future Molly would do the cooking and the staff would eat after the family.

The girls soon had the bed chamber prepared for Martha, and then set about cleaning a room in the attic for themselves. Josie appeared for another bucket of water.

'It's grand up there, miss. We been sharing a room with four others, so real luxury it'll be having one between us.'

'Do you have everything you need?'

'More than what we're used to, thank you kindly, miss. I reckon we'll be done in an hour and be down to help Molly in the kitchen.'

Martha arrived unexpectedly. She was puffing from carrying two bags up the steep track. Demelza hurried out to greet her. 'I didn't think you would arrive so soon. I was about to send Jethro in the cart to fetch you. You should not have had to walk up the hill and carry your own baggage.'

'My dear, I'm fit as a fiddle. See? Hardly out of breath. Now, show me my accommodation and I'll get unpacked.'

'There's no need; we have Josie and Betty to take care of us. We shall be ladies of leisure. I'm hoping when Mr Fairfield is here he won't interfere too much with our lives.'

Martha smiled. 'I've seen the young man about the place. I must say, he seems rather full of himself for a gentleman who travels without a manservant.'

Before Demelza could reply, the boys rushed from the kitchen and threw themselves at Martha. 'Will you tell us a story tonight, Mrs Smith? Please . . . please?' Tom hung onto one hand whilst his brother grabbed the other.

'We'd like the one about the pirates

. . . wouldn't we, Tom?'

'We shall see, boys. Now let me go. I shall drop my bags if you persist.'

The maids appeared and bobbed. 'We'll take your things, madam, if you would care to follow us,' Josie said.

Demelza exchanged smiles with her friend and stepped aside to allow the girls to do their job. Their next task was to prepare chambers for Mr Fairfield, but as he was not arriving until the next morning there was ample time.

Molly was in the kitchen making bread and scones, and Jethro was outside clearing a stall for Mr Fairfield's horse. There was nothing left for Demelza to do.

'Come along, Tom, Jack — let's find your sister and go and see what fruit and vegetables we have ready in the garden today.'

Martha joined them later. 'My dear, I love the room you've given me. I have such a wonderful view right across the bay, and a parlour of my own as well.'

'And no leaks in the ceiling either. I

wish I could say the same for some of the other rooms. We're to have high tea today — scones and cake and cold cuts. I bought fresh ham this morning.'

'But in future the children should eat nursery tea,' Martha said. 'We should dine at five o'clock with Mr Fairfield.'

'Must we? I thought to feed him in the dining room and for us to eat together in the kitchen as usual.'

'Oh no, my dear, he will expect us to dine with him. Do you have an evening gown?'

Demelza giggled. 'I barely have enough clothes to wear during the day. I have one gown that I use for Sundays and that will have to suffice.'

'Didn't you once tell me there's a trunk of material upstairs in the attic? I seem to recall your father brought it back from India or some far off place. Between us I'm sure we could make you something more suitable.'

'In which case, shall we go up there and look whilst there's light enough to see? I have one other gown; Ma made it for me whilst she was bedridden. I've never worn it, but I think it will do.'

* * *

That night the house felt different — no longer quiet and empty — and tomorrow there would be a gentleman residing at Tregorran House again. His chambers were pristine; he would have nothing to complain of. All in all it had been a satisfactory day, Demelza decided when she retired. She'd selected three lengths of material and she and Martha had already cut the pattern for the first gown. It wouldn't be ready for a few days, but she could wear the pretty forget-me-not blue muslin until then.

She woke with the lark but then remembered she now had someone to do her early-morning tasks. She would go down to the beach; the tide would be on the ebb and she could collect mussels and crabs for supper. Molly would have breakfast waiting for the

36

children when they came down, so there was no need to hurry. Their guest was not due until later. She had agreed with Martha that the first meal of the day would be at eight o'clock.

Her bucket was almost full when the distant clang of a bell attracted her attention. This was the signal used in an emergency. She turned and saw Serena waving frantically from the top of the cliff; something must be wrong. She was tempted to abandon her bounty but she'd spent too much effort collecting the shellfish to leave them, however urgent the matter was.

She waved to her sister to indicate she was coming and splashed her way back to the sand. Quickly pushing her feet into her boots, she scrambled up the cliff path, arriving breathless at the top. 'Serena, what's wrong? Has one of the boys had an accident?'

The little girl shook her head; she was jumping up and down. 'No, Melza. Mr Fairfield has arrived and wants to see you. He's ever so handsome, but he's not very friendly. I'm not sure that I like him.'

'I hope you were civil to him, Serena. He's paying a great deal of money to lodge with us and we must ensure he's happy or he might leave.' She could scarcely believe the wretched man had arrived *before* breakfast. Had he done it deliberately in order to catch her out? She wouldn't put it past him one jot. 'Where is he? Is Mrs Smith entertaining him?'

'Molly has put him in the drawing-room and is going to take him a tray of coffee and scones. Mrs Smith isn't down yet and the boys are somewhere in the yard with Jethro.'

Demelza decided to sneak around to the back. With luck she would be able to creep into the kitchen and tidy herself in the scullery before going through to greet Mr Fairfield. However, when she arrived in the yard the boys were dancing around an enormous brown gelding with hooves the size of dinner plates. The beast had laid back ears and his teeth were bared. The boys were about to be savaged.

The horse was tethered to a metal ring in the wall and she could hear Jethro moving about in the barn. She daren't call out in case she startled the animal. Moving swiftly to his head, she spoke soothingly, then reached up and took hold of the bit, smoothing the foam-flecked neck as she did so.

'Boys, move away. Do it at once and do it quietly.'

For once they did as they were told without argument. Her breath hissed through her teeth and she sagged against the horse. Thank God! Her brothers could have been killed by this massive gelding. The noise had alerted Jethro, who limped out from the barn. His smile faded when she explained what had occurred.

'I never knew Bruno was vicious. He seemed quiet enough when I left him. I'm right sorry, miss. I'll make sure I keep the little 'uns away from him in future.'

'See that you do. Tom, Jack, you could have been badly hurt. You must never go near this horse again without supervision, is that quite clear?' They nodded, subdued but apparently not frightened by their narrow escape.

'He didn't like us dancing, did he Tom? I don't think I want a ride on him now. I like Bessie though. Can we talk to her, Melza?' Jack asked.

'Yes, but remember to stay on the fence and not go into the field. I have to go in. Behave yourselves, or you will be confined to your bedroom.'

She was incensed, not with the boys but with the horse's master. As the owner of a dangerous animal, he had a duty to inform her of this fact. She stumbled as one unlaced boot came off — without thinking, she kicked off the other. With her person liberally covered with sand and her hair in disarray, she marched through the kitchen and straight to the drawing-room to confront Mr Fairfield.

3

Lucas was impatient to see the girl who was to be his hostess for the next week or two. He stood at the drawing-room window expectantly; he was not disappointed. Demelza Tregorran emerged from between the gorse bushes with her glorious black hair tumbling around her shoulders and her skirt hitched up, showing her trim ankles and bare feet. Even from this distance she looked lovely.

He had been perfectly comfortable at the village inn, but when the landlady of the Green Man divulged the appalling state of the girl's finances he had decided to transfer to Tregorran House and use some of his unwanted wealth to improve her situation. He certainly didn't want to spend it on himself. He thrust those unwelcome memories aside. Better not to think about the tragic fire that had killed his brother, sister-in-law and their two sons and made him Lord Fairfield — a title he had never expected to inherit and had no intention of using.

This chamber was of good proportions; however, the furniture and curtains were shabby and there were patches of damp on the walls. Tregorran House had once been an impressive dwelling. Smiling slightly, he watched the girl take her sister's hand and run gracefully across the grass. She vanished from sight around the side of the house just as the rattle of crockery heralded the arrival of the promised coffee.

The maid staggered in and carefully placed the tray on a handsome mahogany table. 'Cook thought as you might be a bit peckish, sir, so she's put on fresh bread, butter and conserves. There's also fried ham and eggs. Will you be wanting anything else?'

The girl appeared nervous. His unusual height could be intimidating, especially to Cornish folk who were somewhat smaller than others in the country. 'That looks perfect. Thank you. Will Miss Tregorran be joining me for breakfast?'

'I ain't rightly certain, sir. She's out the back. I reckon as she'll be along soon.'

His earlier irritation that his hostess had not been there to greet him had dissipated. His eagerness to be reacquainted with Miss Tregorran had made him sharp. There was only one cup and saucer; obviously the cook expected him to eat alone. A door slammed and he turned to greet his hostess. His smile of welcome froze as he was confronted by a furious young lady.

★   ★   ★

'Mr Fairfield, you neglected to tell me you owned a dangerous animal when you asked to reside here.'

His mouth thinned and he looked

43

down his nose at her. 'I wasn't aware that I had one. Do I take it Bruno has somehow offended you?'

Demelza barely restrained the impulse to stamp a foot. 'Of course he has. He was about to savage my little brothers. They are only five years of age — '

'Devil take it! I'd no idea you had such young ones living here. Bruno is perfectly amenable to adults and older children but is not reliable with — '

She interrupted him for a second time. 'Exactly what I was telling you. Tom and Jack could have been killed. If you had warned me, I would have told them to stay out of the stable yard.'

'Thank God they weren't injured. I should never have forgiven myself. I beg your pardon, Miss Tregorran. I shall recover my belongings and leave immediately. Consider the remuneration as compensation for almost causing injury to your siblings.'

He was so sincere, her anger

evaporated. 'Please don't blame yourself, sir. The boys are my responsibility and I should have made sure they were not in the way. I don't wish you to leave.'

His smile made her toes curl. 'My dear Miss Tregorran, shall we agree that we are equally responsible and put the matter aside?' He gestured to the laden table. 'There's enough here for a small army. If you haven't already broken your fast, would you do me the honour of joining me?'

Belatedly, she remembered she hadn't stopped to check her appearance and was still without her boots. Blushing an unbecoming shade of scarlet, she shook her head and began to back away. 'No, thank you for asking, but I must — '

His grin disarmed her. 'It's far too late to be concerned about your appearance, my dear. I'm not a man to stand on ceremony. I've spent most of my adult life with the military on the Peninsular and this doesn't allow for such nonsense. Please be seated whilst I ring for another cup and plate.'

Without a by-your-leave, he picked up the brass bell and shook it loudly. Demelza retreated to the far side of the table and pulled out an upright chair. Her stomach rumbled loudly and he raised an eyebrow in her direction. His eyes sparkled but he was polite enough not to comment.

Josie appeared at the door and curtsied. Lucas ordered what was needed and strolled over to join Demelza. She breathed more easily once he was folded onto a chair. He poured her coffee and gestured towards the jug of cream. She nodded and he tipped a generous measure in. 'Here you are. I believe your need is greater than mine. Shall I butter you a slice of bread, or would you like some of the ham and eggs?'

'Both, please. I'm ravenous; I've been up since dawn gathering shellfish from the beach. I hope you like fresh crab and mussel stew?'

Conversation resumed when the tray was all but empty. He sat back with a contented sigh and tossed his napkin on the table. 'That was delicious. Shall we take our coffee outside on the terrace? I expect there are things you wish to tell me and questions you want to ask.'

It was ridiculous to be ushered through the French doors as if she were a society miss and not a simple country girl with bare feet and her hair unpinned. Preoccupied with her thoughts, she failed to take care where she placed her feet and stepped onto a discarded shard of pottery.

She could not hold back an exclamation of pain and dropped to the ground to nurse her injury. Her hands came away blood-stained. She'd done more damage then she'd realised. The next thing she knew, his hands were sliding beneath her and she was in his arms.

'I shall put you on the chaise-longue. No, Miss Tregorran, you will not argue. Let me see what you've done.' He produced a somewhat crumpled hand-kerchief from his pocket and gently wiped away the gore. She flinched even though his touch was feather-light. 'I'm sorry, sweetheart, but I must see if you've broken it.'

She gritted her teeth and allowed him to examine her foot, not sure why she trusted him to do so as he had just told her he was an ex-soldier.

He sat back on his heels. 'I shall need to suture it, but nothing's broken which is fortunate.'

'You're a doctor? You don't look like one.' His amusement made her blush anew. 'I meant, the only physicians of my acquaintance have been elderly.' She stared down at her foot, which was neatly bandaged in his handkerchief. She was concerned to see blood already seeping through.

He laughed. 'All doctors were young once, my dear. And I'm flattered that you consider me so. I am two-and-thirty, considerably older than you, but not yet in my dotage. Remain where you are, keep your foot elevated, and I'll collect what I need from upstairs. Will there be a kettle on the hearth in the kitchen? I need to clean my instruments.'

'I'm sure there is. Don't alarm my brothers and sister. I'd prefer to wait until you have stitched the wound before telling them I've had an accident. I cannot imagine how I came to do so as I'm not normally a clumsy person.'

Whilst resting on the day-bed, she mulled over what she'd learnt about her house-guest. She knew his age and his profession, but not what he was really doing in such a remote part of the country paddling about on the beach. From his diction he was obviously a gentleman, and from his dictatorial behaviour she would surmise he was born to command. She could hardly credit that a man of substance would abandon his responsibilities and wander about in the countryside pretending to paint. There must be more to his story than she knew.

With professional calm and expertise, Mr Fairfield — or rightly, he should be Dr Fairfield — repaired the injury. The experience was painful, but not excruciating, and she'd known at once she was in the hands of an excellent physician.

'There, all done. You must keep off your feet today, but by tomorrow it should be safe enough to hobble about.' He put the used needle and dirty swabs into the basin. 'I'll remove these and wash my hands and then return. We never got to drink our coffee. I shall ask for more to be sent in.'

He was gone before she could call out and tell him that in this house they couldn't afford to waste such a precious commodity just because the drink was cold. The coffee must be reheated or drunk as it was. She was about to swing her feet to the floor when a stabbing pain stopped her. He was right; she had better stay where she was for the moment. The patter of footsteps outside alerted her and she quickly pulled down the hem of her skirt to cover her bandage. Serena arrived first.

'Mr Fairfield says you have stitches in your foot. Can I see them?'

The twins shoved past and rushed across, eager to see this unusual event. 'Us too, Melza! Jack and I want to see your stitches.' Jack reached out to touch the bandage whilst Tom bounced about on the daybed.

'No, children, you must not disturb the dressing,' Lucas said. 'As I explained, your sister's perfectly well. In fact, there's no need for you to be in here at all. You would be better playing outside now you have seen her.'

The children gaped at the speaker. They weren't used to being told what to do so firmly. Demelza bristled; this man took far too much upon himself for a complete stranger, even if he *was* a doctor. 'As I'm perfectly well,' she said, 'I've no objection to them remaining with me. Perhaps *you* have something you might wish to be doing elsewhere?'

Her siblings pressed closer to her. They sensed this giant in their drawing-room was displeased. He stared at them for a second and then nodded, but instead of vanishing as she'd suggested he strode forward. 'Excuse me, little ones; your sister needs to be somewhere she can be undisturbed.'

For the second time in the space of half an hour, Demelza was lifted as if she weighed nothing at all. 'Put me down this instant, Dr Fairfield! What do you think you're doing?'

Ignoring her protest, he grinned down at the watching children. 'Is your sister always so argumentative and stubborn?'

Immediately their demeanour changed and they relaxed, nodding and smiling. Serena spoke for the three of them. 'She never listens, especially not to us.'

Tom rushed over and tugged at her tormentor's coat-tails. 'Are you sending Melza to bed 'cause she's being naughty?'

This was the outside of enough. 'I

insist you put me back on the daybed, Dr Fairfield. I have no wish to be taken anywhere and especially not to my rooms.' When he ignored her and continued on his way to the door, she called out to the children. 'Fetch Mrs Smith immediately. Tell her I need her.'

His hateful laughter echoed around the empty entrance hall. 'I've had the good fortune to meet that redoubtable lady. I'd better get you safely stowed away before she comes to your rescue.' He bounded up the stairs and marched straight to the rear of the building and shouldered his way into her parlour. How did he know where this was? He must have been snooping in her absence.

Betty panted in behind them, her face red and her cap askew. 'Mrs Smith says as you need me, miss.'

Demelza was unceremoniously placed on the chaise-longue. He stepped back, amused by her annoyance. 'Stay here, my dear, and keep your foot raised. I shall make myself scarce, as I can hear trouble approaching.' He waved airily and strolled out just as Martha hurried in.

* * *

Downstairs he was surprised to find the children waiting for him. He ruffled the hair of the two little boys and grinned at the girl. He'd had little to do with youngsters of any sort, but these three seemed an attractive bunch. His nephews had grown up in his absence. If he was to live here for a while it would be as well to get them on his side.

'Children, I know nothing about my temporary home. Why don't you show me around whilst your sister rests her foot?'

With Tom and Jack scampering around him like puppies, he strolled away to be shown the vegetable garden, outbuildings and woodland. No trees grew on the seaward side of the property, but there was a pretty copse on the other side of the brook from which water for the garden and animals was fetched. Signs of neglect were everywhere; fences needed repairing, tiles had slipped and fields were unplanted.

There were some things he could do to help. He'd spent far too long these past months in idleness. Getting his hands dirty — doing some physical work for a change — would suit him.

'Do you grow your own fodder, children?'

'We used to have men in the fields, sir, when our parents werc hcrc and we grew everything we needed,' Serena told him sadly. 'But now we just have hay.'

As he'd thought. All this family needed was financial assistance and they could be self-sufficient once more. He straightened. After several long, bleak months, he finally had a project to occupy him and raise his spirits.

'Well, children, I've enjoyed my tour. At what time do your lessons begin?'

They stared at him as if he were a

nincompoop. Serena smiled. 'We don't have lessons anymore, not since our pa died. Melza's too busy.'

'I see. I believe I overheard your sister and Mrs Smith saying you're to start lessons tomorrow. I suggest you make the most of your last day of freedom.'

'Can we go down to the beach? We have to ask first,' one of the little boys asked.

'If you're careful on the cliff path and don't go into the sea, then I see no reason why not.'

'We like the pools. There's crabs and things in them,' Serena told him.

They didn't need telling a second time, but raced off in the direction of the cliff path. Thank God the dangerous drop was protected by thickly growing gorse bushes. Smiling at their enthusiasm, Lucas wandered back inside, glad he no longer had to duck his head to avoid being knocked unconscious. He was met by Mrs Smith, who nodded frostily.

'Dr Fairfield, what have you done with the children? Miss Tregorran is anxious to know their whereabouts. They are not permitted to wander freely about the place.'

'They have been showing me around the estate and now they have gone down to the beach.'

'I suppose that's in order. In future, sir, could you inform either Miss Tregorran or myself if you're taking the children anywhere.'

'I shall do so, of course. I'm afraid I told them lessons would be resuming soon. I overheard your conversation with Miss Tregorran on the subject.'

Her rigid posture relaxed somewhat. 'Excellent. I rather think their sister has been putting off telling them. We've agreed I shall set up the school room and take over their education. There's nothing I like better than directing young minds.' She nodded and then ran with a remarkable agility up the stairs. He followed her, intending to collect his easel and watercolours. Today was a perfect day to paint and the view from the cliff top would be spectacular.

A year ago the idea of idling his time away in such a frivolous pastime would have appalled him. He had been working as a medic with Wellington's army — then everything changed. He blinked and scrubbed his eyes dry. Losing his entire family had been almost too much to bear.

His apartment was at the front of the building, but he heard the exclamation of horror coming from Miss Tregorran quite clearly. Forgetting he was in bad odour with both women, he ran to the door.

★   ★   ★

'How could he be so stupid as to let them go down when the tide's rising? I have to go and get them.' Demelza was attempting to scramble up when the doctor's strong hands pressed on her shoulders, holding her still.

'Remain where you are; I should have

58

realised. I'll go and fetch them myself,' he said.

'Demelza, my dear girl,' Martha said, 'what harm can they come to? Surely they'd have more sense than to go down if the tide's coming in? After all, they have been born and bred on the coast.'

'That's the problem, Martha. They know they're not allowed down on the beach to play in the rock pools unless it's safe. Dr Fairfield gave them permission. They'll assume the tide is going out.'

He didn't wait to hear more. His cheeks paled beneath his tan and he raced from the room. His heavy footsteps could be heard throughout the house.

'Martha, help me to the window. Goodness, the bell! He must take that with him. The children will come back immediately if they hear it ringing.' Fortunately, the window was open. Demelza stuck her head through just as he emerged below them. 'Dr Fairfield, take the bell by the front door. Ring it and the children will know it's an emergency.'

He snatched it up and raced for the cliff path. He'd discarded his topcoat and waistcoat and was in his shirt sleeves. Despite her anxiety, she couldn't help noticing his athletic build and the way his long legs covered the ground. He paused at the cliff edge and rang the bell. She held her breath. He turned and waved and then vanished between the bushes.

'Thank the Lord, the children are safe. Martha, I'm not sure that man should remain here. That's twice today he's put their lives in danger and caused more upset than we've had in months.'

'Don't fret, my dear girl. I'm sure Dr Fairfield will be more careful in future. He's obviously not accustomed to having children around him. He's a bachelor, which is fortuitous, don't you think?'

Demelza knew where this conversation was leading and hastily changed the subject. 'As I'm confined to my chamber for the next day, I'll occupy myself stitching my new evening gown.' She hopped back to the day bed and flopped down. 'I'd quite forgotten how many bolts of material there were in the attic, and such lovely patterns too.'

'Indeed, my dear, you will hardly know yourself once your new garments are completed and the house brought back to life. Please forgive me, but I must return to the school room. I have commandeered Josie and Betty to help me clean. You wouldn't believe how much dust has accumulated since the room was last in use.'

★ ★ ★

The children looked round when Lucas rang the bell. They began to replace their stockings and boots. Dropping the bell at the top of the steep path, he descended with more speed than dignity. He arrived in a cloud of sand and pebbles just as they ran up.

'Is there something amiss, sir?' Serena enquired politely.

'No, not now. The tide's coming in. I shouldn't have given you permission to come down here.'

The boys spun and stared at the sea with open mouths. He watched them move closer, seeking comfort from each other. 'Your sister is waiting anxiously. We must return at once and reassure her you're quite safe.'

The girl set off ahead of them, but the little ones seemed rooted to the spot. He bent and scooped them up. 'Come along, lads. One of you on my back, and the other my front.' His unexpected action had the desired effect and, giggling and wriggling, they arranged themselves to his satisfaction. 'Hang on tight; I shall take this at a run.'

He emerged at the cliff top and immediately looked up at the chamber window from which Demelza had been watching. She was no longer there; she must have understood his earlier gesture. He noticed the bell leaning drunkenly against a gorse bush. 'Right, which of you is on my back?'

'Jack. I'm Jack.'

'Jack, when I bend down you must stretch out and pick up the bell. If you fall off you will lose a point.'

Tom tugged at his shirt collar. 'What's *a point?* Have I got one to lose as well?'

Wishing he'd never mentioned the subject, Lucas tried to explain. 'It's a game, boys. We all started off with ten points and the person with the most left at the end of the day will get a prize.'

Serena gazed up anxiously. 'Can I join in this game, or is it just for you and the boys?'

'The game's for all of us. Your sister has lost five points for being silly enough to cut her foot. I have lost all my points already. You three have still to lose one. Are you ready, Jack?'

Somehow the child managed to retrieve the bell and stay *in situ*. Lucas was beginning to enjoy himself. 'Well done. Now it's your turn, Serena. I will race you to the house. If I win, you lose two points.'

Squealing with excitement, she raced away. He followed, appearing to make every effort to overtake, but hanging back to allow her to win. He dropped the boys in a heap on the grass. 'I'm quite exhausted after all that. Does anyone know where I can get a cold drink of water?'

Chattering like magpies, the children led him around the house to the kitchen yard where there was a pump. 'Right. Tom, you pull the handle and I'll put my head underneath.' Lucas slipped off his shirt and ducked under the spout.

After a deal of heaving and laughter, water eventually emerged. The icy deluge made him splutter. He shook himself and then wiped his face on his shirt. The children were staring at him in horror. What had he done now to alarm them?

4

'What is it Serena?' Lucas asked.

She shook her head. 'Demelza doesn't like us to use our clothes to dry ourselves.'

Jack joined in. 'She doesn't. She'll be cross with you and you won't have any points left.'

Lucas grinned. 'I've already lost them. Your sister won't be cross, young man. It's my shirt and I can do as I please with it. These rules only apply to you two and your sister.'

The other boy bounced. 'Can we share your rules, then, sir?'

'We'll see.' He shrugged his damp shirt on over his head. 'Come on, little ones. I'm sure there's more you can show me.'

At noon he escorted his adoring flock back to the house for their mid-day meal. The delicious aroma of cooking mackerel filled the kitchen. A dish of potatoes sprinkled with chopped parsley and glistening with butter stood proudly in the centre of the table. Next to this was a bowl of salad leaves and radishes. Lucas smiled at the sprinkling of marigold petals; they certainly looked pretty and presumably were safe to eat. There was no sign of the cook or the maids. Should he remove the fish from the spit?

Serena answered this question for him. 'Uncle Lucas, the fish are burning.'

Grasping the hot skewers with two cloths, he carefully transferred them from the fire to the table. His mouth watered and his stomach gurgled loudly. The children giggled. 'As you no doubt heard, I am starving. I hope some of these are for me.'

The cook appeared from the scullery and seemed put out to find him in the kitchen. 'I have laid up for you in the dining room, sir. If you would care to go through, one of the girls will serve you right away.'

'I would prefer to eat here with the children, Mrs Trewith, but will dine elsewhere.'

Once they were all seated the cook removed the largest fish from the skewer and served him first. The skin was crisp, the white flesh firm and succulent. He knew it would taste as delicious as it looked.

'Help yourself to potatoes and salad, sir. Now, children, I hope you're hungry, for there's plenty to go round.'

* * *

Demelza was eagerly anticipating her mid-day meal. Martha was to join her, but the children would eat in the kitchen. Poor Molly was obliged to prepare meals and have them delivered to three different places today. Josie arrived with the tray, bursting to pass on some gossip.

'Do you know, miss, the gentleman is eating in the kitchen with the children. Molly asked him right politely to go into the dining room, but he wouldn't budge. She ain't too pleased about it, I can tell you.'

Demelza laughed. She could just imagine Molly's outrage. Within a few hours of her arrival she had taken over the running of the house. Demelza supposed she should protest, but it was such a luxury not having all the household decisions to make.

'Josie, we don't stand on ceremony at Tregorran House and I am pleased Dr. Fairfield is of the same mind. Now, could you fetch Mrs. Smith from the school room or this delicious repast will be cold.'

* * *

The pleasure of stitching her new gown had long paled when a soft knock on the door disturbed her. The children were playing cricket on the grass with Martha so it couldn't be one of them. Her fingers clenched and she stabbed her thumb with the needle. Before she had time to invite him in, Dr Fairfield was inside. Hastily she stuffed the partially stitched evening gown under a convenient pillow, trusting no blood from her thumb had spoilt the Indian silk.

'Another injury, Miss Tregorran? I shall begin to believe you are decidedly accident-prone.' He strolled across and, picking up a chair, spun it and straddled the seat. He folded his arms across the top and smiled at her disarmingly.

Whatever she'd been about to say was forgotten. Her heart beat faster and her cheeks glowed. 'I must thank you for entertaining the children this morning. I can't remember the last time I heard them laughing so uproariously.' She pursed her lips and attempted to look fierce. 'However, I'm most displeased to have been told I had five points deducted from my total when I wasn't aware I was part of the game.'

His eyes flashed and his lips curved.

'I'm afraid, my dear, that I must deduct a further point for your misuse of a needle.'

She couldn't restrain a bubble of mirth. 'It's the most nonsensical game I've ever heard of. Who is the arbitrator? For what are points lost and gained?'

'I've no idea; I've never played any sort of game before. The children have taken my suggestion and turned it into their own challenge. It would seem the rules are simple: points are deducted if you injure yourself or do anything you shouldn't.' He rested his chin on his hands. 'I've already lost all mine.' His eyes twinkled. 'In fact, I believe I've lost tomorrow's quota as well.'

'Good heavens! Whatever did you do?'

'I dried myself with my shirt.'

Demelza tingled all over as an image of him half naked popped unbidden into her head. 'Oh dear! Such a misdemeanour definitely deserves to have five points deducted from your total.'

His answering smile added to her discomposure. 'The children are the best judges of their own misbehaviour. This game should benefit us all.'

Demelza belatedly recalled he must have come to visit her for a purpose. 'Dr Fairfield, was there something you wish to speak to me about?'

'It seems that I must dine in solitary splendour. I was wondering if I might be permitted to assist you downstairs so all three of us can share the meal.'

She had intended to refuse but said something quite the reverse. 'I should like that, sir. I'm already bored by my confinement up here. Serving dinner in one place will make life much easier for the staff as well.'

In one fluid movement he rose, returned the chair and strolled to the open door. 'I shall not dress for dinner tonight.' He nodded solemnly. 'In fact, I shall not dress for dinner any night as I don't have my evening rig with me. By the by, I have to go to Plymouth next week. You and Mrs Smith must make a list of any purchases you require and I'll return with them.'

'Will you be away for long?' For some reason the thought of his absence depressed her.

'A week at the most, hopefully less than that. I shall leave you to your stitching, Miss Tregorran, and return at five o'clock to collect you.'

With a casual wave he was gone; the room seemed strangely empty afterwards. Heartily sick of sewing — although it was usually one of her favourite pastimes — she stretched out and rang the brass bell Martha had left for her use. Eventually Betty puffed in.

'Good. I'm sorry to drag you away from whatever you were doing, but I've an urgent task for you. Somewhere in the back of my closet is a forget-me-not blue muslin. Please have it ready for me to wear tonight.' She ran her fingers through her hair. It felt sticky; high time she washed it. 'I wish to wash my hair, and I'll have to do it in my dressing-room. Could you ask Mrs Trewith to send up as much hot water as she can spare?'

'Lawks, miss, you'll not do that without help, with it being so long and all. I'll do it for you, then you can sit on the window seat in the sunshine and I reckon it'll be dry in no time.'

Good heavens, even Betty was giving her instructions now. This was a new experience for her, but not an unpleasant one. Having sole charge of the household for so long, and constantly worrying about making ends meet, had been debilitating. Now she could relax and pretend she was a wealthy young lady with nothing at all to do. Sometimes she felt old beyond her years, nearer *his* age than her own of just two-and-twenty.

* * *

Martha arrived promptly at five o'clock wearing the same plain grey cotton dress. 'I can't tell you how relieved I am we're not going to have to dress formally in the evenings. I've no time for such nonsense.' She smiled at Demelza. 'My dear girl, you look quite beautiful. You should wear a pretty gown and put your hair up more often.'

'Thank you, I think.' She grinned. 'I'm always so busy, I never have time to worry about my appearance. However, I think I might enjoy acting the part of a lady for a while.' She shook out the folds of her skirt and smiled ruefully at her bare toes. 'I considered wearing stockings but I only have two pairs without holes and don't intend to spoil either of them.'

'Not to worry. Your foot will be much better without the constriction. Molly has been banging about in a frenzy all afternoon. I hope she's up to the task of cooking for so many.'

'She used to cook at The Green Man when Old Jenny owned it. I'm sure running *my* kitchen will be simplicity itself after that.' Demelza glanced down at the revealing neckline of her gown. 'I feel quite naked with so much of me on show, but this is the only one I've got that's suitable. Whenever we used the dining room Ma insisted we changed into our Sunday best.'

'My dear, that's positively modest compared with some I've seen. I must say the dining room looks splendid. I took the liberty of picking an armful of flowers for the silver epergne. That magnificent table just cried out for a centrepiece.'

Their conversation was cut short by the arrival of Dr Fairfield. He paused, filling the doorway, and his eyes darkened. Then he bowed and smiled, at his most charming, and Demelza thought she'd imagined the strange expression. She was relieved to see he'd done no more than brush his hair and put on a fresh cravat.

'Miss Tregorran, I see you're ready. Shall we go down?'

Now the time had come to be moved, Demelza wished she had refused. As he bent to slip his arm around her waist she inhaled his scent, a mix of lemon soap and salt. Reluctantly, she threaded her arm through his. A strange sensation rippled through her and she pressed her burning cheek into his shoulder.

Martha walked beside them, making sure no liberties were taken. Demelza was helped through the house to the freshly polished dining room and gently placed on a waiting chair. It took her a moment to recover her composure. She looked around with delight.

'Oh, what a transformation a bit of beeswax and some flowers can make to a room. I can't remember the last time this chamber looked so pleasing.' She carefully avoided making eye contact with the doctor.

'Tregorran is a beautiful building, my dear. High time your home was brought back to life,' Martha said.

Chairs scraped as her companions were seated. 'Tomorrow I intend to start repairing the roof,' Lucas said. 'It took me the whole of today to gather the materials and assistance I'll need.'

Demelza risked a glance in his direction. 'There's no need for you to do that, sir.'

'I hate to contradict a lady, but there's every need. Another storm like the one we had the other night and you might well lose a couple of ceilings.'

'But you're a paying guest. I intend to use some of your rent to employ local men to do the repairs. I can't allow you to put yourself out in this way.'

'Nonsense; I've grown bored with painting and sketching and can't wait to do something useful. You'll be doing me a favour, Miss Tregorran.'

She was about to protest again when Martha interrupted her. 'I take it roof-mending is another of your many skills, sir? How is it that you have been a physician, an artist and also worked as a labourer?'

The question hung in the air. His eyes narrowed with annoyance and Demelza braced herself. 'I should tell you to mind your own business, madam, but that would be uncivil, would it not?' Even the redoubtable Martha looked uncomfortable as he pinned her with his icy stare. 'However, I can see I'll have no peace until you are both fully cognizant of my situation. I was a medic in Wellington's army until my brother and his entire family died in a devastating house fire.'

His throat convulsed and Demelza saw the glitter of tears in his eyes. He recovered immediately and continued, his voice commendably steady. 'I was forced to resign my commission and return to take care of things. My family home is a blackened ruin. Those that I loved have been torn from this world. I cannot bear to be at my ancestral home so here I am pretending to be an artist.'

'I'm so sorry for your loss,' Demelza said. 'Please feel free to mend anything you like if it helps you deal with your grief. And you are welcome to stay here as long as you wish.'

His lopsided smile made her heart

somersault. 'I thank you, Miss Tregorran. I had feared you might send me packing after this afternoon's incident.'

'I did consider it, but decided to be practical.'

Martha dabbed her eyes with the corner of her napkin. 'Might I enquire why you are travelling as plain Mr Fairfield?'

He ran a finger around his neck cloth as if the question made him uncomfortable. He shrugged. 'That life is over. I must eventually assume my responsibilities and return to Hampshire. I have a competent estate manager taking care of things in my absence but I cannot remain away indefinitely. The house will have to be rebuilt, architects employed . . . that's not something I can leave to anyone else.'

'Shall we refer to you as Dr Fairfield, or Mr Fairfield in future?' Martha asked.

'You must suit yourself, Mrs Smith. It's a matter of indifference to me. Ah — is that the sound of food arriving?'

'We are having crab patties, tarragon sauce and fresh cooked prawns. Strawberries and cream to follow,' Martha informed them as Josie and Betty came in with steaming tureens. Molly, who was for the present both housekeeper and cook, trotted in behind to ensure the girls served correctly.

Lucas smiled at Molly. 'This looks and smells delicious.'

'They'll be back with the tatties, spinach and carrots,' Molly said. 'There's fresh bread and butter to mop up the sauce. The cider's good and cold; Jethro hung the jug in the well for an hour or two.'

Demelza hid her amusement as her guests exchanged glances. Molly did take a deal of getting used to. Soon the girls had completed their journeys and the table was groaning under the weight of their supper.

'This looks absolutely splendid. As we are dining informally, shall we help ourselves?' Martha enquired. Demelza nodded and reached out with the serving spoon but her hand collided with Lucas's. The spoon dropped into the dish of vegetables, scattering carrots across the table.

Laughing, he retrieved the spoon and scooped up the debris. 'I beg your pardon. Allow me to serve you *without* throwing the food all over the place.'

'Thank you, but you can have those that were on the table. I fear they'll taste of polish.'

Martha took charge. 'I shall dish up, Demelza. I don't wish to have my meal scattered before I eat it.'

Several helpings later, Lucas finally pushed away his plate with a groan. 'I can eat no more. I don't think I've eaten better anywhere in the world.'

Suddenly, Martha clapped her hand to her mouth. 'I believe crabmeat disagrees with me. Excuse me — '

She ran from the room, leaving them alone. Demelza dropped her cutlery and prepared to follow. Lucas reached out and touched her hand. 'No, sweetheart, Mrs Smith does not require you. A bilious attack is best dealt with alone. Don't look so worried. I shall go up in a while and check she's not in any serious distress.'

'If you're sure, then I'll remain here.' His smile sent her pulse racing. She leant forward to recover her dropped napkin. Instantly his eyes darkened and a hectic flush appeared along his cheekbones. She sat back sharply. She recognised that expression. Was he reacting to her low-cut gown? Her cheeks were as red as his.

He slammed back his chair and grabbed the empty cider jug. 'I need another drink; I'll fetch some from the pantry.'

The dining room was too stuffy. She needed to cool her burning cheeks outside. Using the furniture to lean on, she hobbled onto the terrace. Childish shrieks of laughter disturbed the night. The children were returning from the beach, where they had gone with Josie after tea. She wished she could go and meet them. The less time she spent alone with her guest, the better it would be for both of them.

How could a gentleman she'd known for barely a day be causing her so much disquiet?

The grass was damp beneath her feet, the blackbirds and thrushes trilling their goodnight song. Not an evening for worrying. Tonight she would think only that with Lucas's help they would lead a more comfortable life. She waved and her siblings rushed over, their buckets rattling with the mussels they'd collected.

'I'll take them buckets through to Molly, miss,' Josie said. 'Then I'll get them all to bed.'

'Off you go children. I'm afraid Mrs Smith is unwell, so you'll have to forego your story tonight.' She kissed them fondly and they skipped away with Josie.

Where was her dinner companion? Surely it couldn't take so long to find a jug of cider. The silvery light of the full moon transformed the garden into a place of enchantment, but she didn't wish to experience it alone. Deciding to return, she turned and collided with his solid bulk as he was coming out. For a moment they rocked from side to side. His arms gripped her waist as he fought to keep them both from falling.

The heat from his hands was spreading. A delicious warmth slowly engulfed her. What was happening? Was it *she* who was now going down with a summer fever?

5

Lucas regained his balance but seemed reluctant to release her. Demelza pressed against his chest; his shirt was gaping open and her fingertips brushed his naked flesh. With a squeak of shock she recoiled and this time he let her go.

'If you're quite ready, Demelza, I've been growing roots inside waiting for you.' His gentle teasing restored her composure. Forgetting she was unable to walk properly, she put down her injured foot and yelped. 'Botheration, I do so hate being incapacitated in this way.'

'Idiot child, you should not be out here. I shall have to carry you.'

Indignant at his casual reference to her maturity, she scowled. 'Dr Fairfield. I would rather hop than be carried about like a parcel.'

'Then allow me to assist you as I did

earlier. It's far too hot to go inside. I thought we could sit and watch the sea from the path.'

Somewhat mollified by his suggestion, she stopped protesting and once again he placed his arm around her waist. Together, they made their way to the cliff edge.

'I should like that, but would prefer to go down to the beach. Obviously I can't do that tonight.' The booming of the waves below confirmed her comment.

'Is it safe to walk on the beach at high tide? Will there be sand showing?'

'Yes — but only a yard or two. That's why I have to be cautious when allowing the children down there by themselves. However, unless the sea's rough, it's usually safe to land a boat or lead a pony through the shallows.' Why was he looking so fierce? 'Do you know, it's perfectly possible to walk to the village along the beach. It would take far longer . . . '

He gripped her arm. 'Are you saying

smugglers use your beach at night?'

'Of course they do, but infrequently and only when the revenue officers are patrolling their normal haunts. They always leave me a gift of some sort. Where do you think the brandy came from?' His fingers were tense on her wrist. Why should something as natural as smuggling bother him?

'A girl alone should not have dealings with such men. You're placing yourself and the little ones in extreme danger.'

She snatched her arm back. 'You know nothing of the matter. Stopping them is likely to be more dangerous. And anyway, most of them are fishermen from the village and have known me since I was in leading strings. I expect there are bands elsewhere with murderous intent, but not here.'

'So they never bother you? They don't come anywhere near the house?'

'Good heavens, no. Round here things work differently; when there's to be a patrol a warning is sent and that's when they use *this* cove. This means the two groups never come face to face, but you would be surprised how much is washed ashore from passing ships for the revenue men to find.'

'So if they're apprehended they give up without a fight? No officers are ever injured?' His laugh sent shivers down her spine. 'A perfect arrangement; let's hope the authorities don't get to hear about it and send someone who puts his duty before his purse to take charge of the patrols.'

Her amusement faded as she recalled the unwelcome incomers in the village. Was her peaceful co-existence with the smugglers about to end?

Immediately his expression changed to one of concern. 'Miss Tregorran, are you worried about your roof?' She shook her head. 'What is it? Tell me. Something is bothering you.'

'It's neither the roof nor the village smugglers — both are part of my life. I'm worried that something more pernicious has come to Tregorran.' Should she confide in him? After all, he was little more than a stranger. She glanced up. He was reassuringly solid; exactly the sort of man who would know how to deal with the men from Polperro.

'Two weeks ago some ruffians moved into an empty cottage in the village. Since then there has been talk . . . talk of a second group of free-traders. These are ferocious men. Unlike Old Johnny, they will kill to protect their contraband.'

'Good grief! That's far more serious. Are you certain these rumours are true?'

'I've seen the men with my own eyes. When I was in the village yesterday there was a menacing atmosphere and men I've known for years refused to meet my eye.'

'Nothing more definite than a feeling?'

She bristled. He doubted her word. 'Dr Fairfield, I can assure you, I know my own people well enough to detect a change in their demeanour.'

'I beg your pardon, my dear. As these villains are unlikely to appear on your beach tonight, shall we forget about them for the present?'

'Very well. Will you give me your word you will investigate for me tomorrow? I fear there will be bloodshed if these men are not rooted out and sent on their way. Smuggling is illegal, but unfortunately without this income many of the villagers would starve.'

'Are you suggesting it's permissible for local men to use your beach for landing their ill-gotten gains, but not for strangers to do so?'

'Sir, I've explained how things work in Tregorran. Outsiders will bring danger and disaster in their wake. Surely you don't wish to see things escalate into violence?'

'I've no desire to see any form of illegal activity. However, I promise to wander down to The Green Man and see what I can discover.'

'Thank you. That's all I ask of you. I

feel responsible for the deprivations in the village. In former times our family supplied both employment and food to anyone in need. If my suspicions are proved correct I'll inform Squire Reynolds. He will soon see them off.'

His smile was wide. 'I take it your local magistrate is also involved with Old Johnny's gang?'

Having such a conversation whilst half-hopping across the grass was ridiculous. Thank goodness the cliff edge was just ahead. 'Look, can you see the lighter gap? That's the path,' Demelza said.

Lucas kept his arm around her waist to steady her. He seemed as eager as she to change the subject. 'It's a spectacular setting. Have your family lived here for many generations? Presumably the village is named after you and not the other way round.'

'It certainly is. A hundred years ago we were wealthy; my ancestors owned the village and the fishing fleet. Things are different now. My grandfather was obliged to sell the cottages to another gentleman in order to pay off his gambling debts. We have sunk further and further into penury over the years.'

'Then I shall make it my business to put things right before I leave. No, I shall not be dissuaded. Allow me to spend my unwanted fortune as I please. Let something good come from my family tragedy.' His voice was so bleak, her eyes filled and she sniffed. 'You're becoming chilled; we must return to the house immediately.' He laughed quietly. 'No, please don't argue, I'm a medical man and I know of what I speak.'

She relaxed into his embrace, enjoying the unusual sensation of someone taking care of her for a change. He guided her straight into the drawing-room. 'There, let me look at your foot. I imagine the dressing will be dirty and need changing before you retire.' He dropped to his haunches and picked up her foot.

His hands sliding across her ankle made her light-headed with excitement.

This would not do; she must remain aloof from him. There was no future in the relationship, for as soon as he recovered from his grief he would be gone. And anyway, a gentleman such as he would never consider marrying a girl like her. She shoved him away with her undamaged foot and he tumbled backwards onto his backside. His look of astonishment made her laugh out loud.

'I beg your pardon, but I don't require you to act as my abigail. I can assure you I'm quite capable of changing my own dressing if needs be.' Before he could stop her, she hopped nimbly to the door and out into the entrance hall. She viewed the stairs with disfavour, then realised she could ascend quite easily if she did so on one knee.

At any moment she expected him to erupt from the chamber and snatch her into the air, but she was able to complete her undignified journey without his help. She reached the sanctuary of her own apartment without interference and was surprised, but delighted, to find Betty waiting to act as her abigail.

*　*　*

Lucas jack-knifed and flopped into the dilapidated armchair. Not only her beauty, but her lively wit and courage set his pulses racing. There was something about this girl that was drawing him in. How many young ladies in her position would have managed to keep the family together these past few years? The sound of her bumping up the stairs made him smile. He must let her go alone. Just being near her was a temptation he found increasingly difficult to resist.

He swore out loud. He had no option but to return and try to rebuild his home and assume an unwanted life as a lord and gentlemen of means. She was irrevocably linked to Tregorran House. When he left for Plymouth, if he had any sense he would not return here. If he did, he could only see heartache ahead for both of them. Damn it! There was now his rash promise to investigate the unwanted extra smugglers, as well as repair the house and sort out the family's finances. He couldn't depart until that was done.

*　*　*

Demelza tossed restlessly, unable to settle. From whichever way she viewed the situation, she could see no happy solution. From disliking her house-guest intensely, her feelings had changed until she was a fair way to falling in love with him. How could this have happened so quickly? This emotion was new to her. When it came to gentlemen, she was quite ignorant. Ma had discouraged young men from calling, and after her mother's death she had been too busy taking care of the family to think about affairs of the heart.

If she looked at the issue dispassion-
ately, she could see that what had
happened was inevitable. When a
handsome man moved into the home of
an unattached lady of impressionable
years, what could one expect? Good
heavens! She sat up, wide awake, as
something quite extraordinary occurred
to her. Martha was a woman of the
world, had moved in polite society and
knew how things worked. She must
have been well aware this could come
about and was positively encouraging it.

She collapsed on the pillows, scarcely
able to draw breath as excitement and
anticipation rippled through her. Fate
had sent her to the beach and thrown
her in his path. She smiled in the
darkness; it would be more true to say
that *he* had been pitched into *her* path.
If Martha approved, and thought she
was a suitable partner for a gentleman
as grand as Dr Fairfield, then who was
she to cavil? Could she call him by his
given name in the privacy of her
thoughts? Daringly, she resumed her

musing. Lucas seemed as affected by her presence as she was by his. Perhaps the good Lord had sent him to Tregorran especially for her.

Even the unwelcome arrival of the Polperro men no longer seemed as bothersome. After all, had not Lucas agreed to investigate? On that happy thought she fell asleep.

* * *

Demelza was not surprised, when roused next morning by Betty pulling back the curtains, that her dreams had been filled with images of a tall fair-haired gentleman with periwinkle-blue eyes.

'Mornin', miss. Mrs Smith says I'm to stay and help you dress. Is there anything special you wants me to get out for you?'

'Anything that's not too worn or faded. I don't think there's a large selection. Whatever time is it? Have I overslept?'

'The master said you was to be left to

sleep and that you was to stay up here today. I don't reckon it's more than eight o'clock. The little ones are washed and dressed and eating breakfast in the kitchen. Mrs Smith says as lessons will start promptly at eight-thirty every morning.'

Demelza felt a surge of anger. First *he* ran roughshod over her position in the household. This was bad enough, but at least *he* was a paying guest, which did give him some rights. Was she invisible? No longer mistress of Tregorran House, but relegated to the position of a delicate female?

Her silly fantasies of the previous night vanished and common sense reasserted itself. 'Kindly assist me to my closet. I care not what I put on as long as it's clean and serviceable. Somewhere on one of the shelves you'll find some pattens that I use in the winter. I believe they will allow me to go downstairs without difficulty.' She pursed her mouth and dared the girl to contradict.

'Right away, Miss Tregorran. You'll not be wanting your breakfast on a tray, then?'

'Certainly not. When you have finished your duties here make sure you pay particular attention to Dr Fairfield's apartment. Without his rent I could not afford to employ you here.'

Twenty minutes later she had negotiated the stairs and was on her way to the kitchen. She wished to set matters straight there before seeking out the man she had for a fleeting moment imagined might be her future husband. A handsome face was not sufficient to make a happy marriage. A dictatorial gentleman would not make a comfortable partner, however noble his motives. She was too used to doing things her own way. Tregorran House was *her* domain, her brothers' birthright, and no one — not even Lucas Fairfield — was going to take it away from her.

Molly threw up her floury hands when Demelza hobbled in to the kitchen. 'Well, my lovely, I never did expect to see you down today. You'll not find the children here. They was that eager to begin their lessons, they dashed off right quickly.'

'I wish to speak to Dr Fairfield. Have you any notion where he is?'

'I reckon he's outside somewhere. There's men from the village come to mend the roof. Listen, don't you hear that banging?'

Disappointed she had accomplished neither of her objectives, Demelza pulled out a chair and sat waiting for her own meal. The repast was served in silence, her unexpected appearance making her normally garrulous cook work quietly for a change. Demelza pushed her food around her plate, as she had no appetite this morning.

'Molly, I would like you to come to the small parlour with your suggestions for today's menu. We also need to discuss how best to use Josie; I should like Betty to become abigail to both myself and Mrs Smith. Also, we must find you a kitchen maid to help in here.'

'I know just the girl. Her pa died last year and her ma's married again and she don't get on with him. Mary's her name; she's not much older than Serena and will be glad to have a safe place to live.'

'Good. We shall discuss this later on. I think, Molly, that perhaps you should refer to my siblings more formally. Mrs Smith and Dr Fairfield will expect this.'

The atmosphere in the kitchen changed. Neither Molly nor Jethro were used to remaining within the bounds of propriety. Would they be able to behave as she wanted?

'Very well, Miss Tregorran. I'll let my Jethro know he's to mind his manners in future.'

The clatter on the roof intensified. Demelza decided she would go out onto the grass in front of the house and see what was going on. Molly kneaded the dough on the table with unnecessary force.

'I'll be serving all your meals in the

dining room in future, Miss Tregorran. No need for you to come into my kitchen any more. I'll be along to see you in an hour.'

Oh dear! Now Molly was displeased with her. Should she not have spoken? She made her way through the house at snail's pace, allowing her time to take in the improvements already made. The floor boards gleamed; the stairs and banisters shone enough to see one's face in. Before long her home would be pristine and sparkling. What a shame there wasn't the wherewithal to replace the dilapidated furniture and thread-bare hangings.

The sun was not at its zenith but already the air was hot. Heaven knew what it must be like on the roof. She moved slowly across the weed-filled turning circle and stopped when she was several yards away. She still couldn't see who was making the din, so backed up slowly until the workman was revealed.

Her shock was so great, her heel

caught in the hem of her dress and the next thing she knew she was spread-eagled on the ground. Even from there she could see Lucas in nothing but his breeches and boots busily hammering fresh timber across one of the gaping holes in the roof. He was magnificent. His naked shoulders gleamed in the sunlight; his muscles rippled; his long, lean thighs braced to hold him steady. In all her life she'd never seen anything so beautiful. He was like a statue she'd seen in a travel book her father had brought back from Italy.

Slowly she pushed herself up on her elbows, her breath ragged, unable to pull her gaze away. A rattle at the school room window drew her attention. Her siblings were hanging out. Martha's face appeared beside them and her strident voice echoed across the lawn.

'My dear girl, how unfortunate. Did you catch your foot? Do you need me to come down and help you up?'

To her consternation, Lucas heard

the shout and looked over. He straightened and moved like a cat to the edge of the roof. One might have thought he was fully clothed, not half-dressed like an urchin on the beach. 'Sweetheart, are you injured? You shouldn't be downstairs, I gave instructions you should remain inside and rest your injury.'

His words prompted her to scramble up, her cheeks flaming not just with embarrassment but also indignation. She glared up at him. 'I trod on my hem. I'm perfectly well, thank you both for asking. However, as you are both listening, I shall speak plainly.'

His grin all but deterred her. 'Shout plainly, I think you mean, my dear. Do go ahead. I have nothing better to do than hang onto the roof thirty feet above the ground and listen to your words of wisdom.'

'You are the most infuriating gentleman I've ever met. It would serve you right if you fell off and broke your neck.' Good heavens, what devil had made her say something so ridiculous? 'Oh, botheration, get on with your work and stop issuing orders as if you were master of this house.'

Her words caused him to lose his grip and he slithered down the slates until his boots jammed in the gutter. Her breath hissed through her teeth. He could have fallen and it would have been her fault. What was the matter with her? She was renowned for her good humour and tolerance, and within the space of two days she was behaving like a veritable shrew.

'I'm so sorry, Dr Fairfield. I didn't mean to startle you. I have a headache and must go inside out of the sun.' Ignoring the shocked faces at the school room window, she half ran, half hopped, into the house. Her heart was hammering. Had a stone somehow lodged in her throat? He could have been killed. The enormity of what had almost happened overwhelmed her and her eyes brimmed.

Like an old lady she made her way to

the pretty yellow sitting-room her mother had once used. She collapsed into an armchair to wait for her composure to return. How could someone she'd known for scarcely any time at all have turned her life upside-down? If she was honest, his appearance made her heart beat faster. The fact that his mouth turned up at the corners and there were endearing wrinkles on either side of his eyes was a constant source of fascination. The way he teased her and called her 'sweetheart' drew her to him.

Sweetheart? Why was he larding his conversation with such endearments? She'd heard him address Serena like this. Did this mean he viewed her as a child as well? Then, as if she had fallen flat on her face in the sea, sanity returned. She understood his motives. He was an army doctor; it had been his job to protect and help those in need. She and her family were his project. He didn't view her as a prospective bride but as another child in need of his care and guidance.

Well, she would soon put him right on that score. Tonight she would demonstrate she was no child, but a woman grown and able to take care of herself and her family without his interference.

6

Lucas shuffled up the roof, relieved Demelza had vanished as she was a dangerous distraction. He reclaimed his hammer and knocked in a couple of nails with excessive force. Damn it! This wouldn't do. He was behaving like a green boy, not a mature man of experience. He must step back — keep his distance — before he did something reprehensible.

In future he would dine in the village, for being closeted with a lovely young lady every night was asking for trouble. His hammer slipped through his fingers and vanished into the hole he'd been repairing. He swore loudly. The two labourers repairing the plaster below him grinned. One put down his tools and picked up the item.

'You want this back, sir?'

'No, thank you. I'm done here, lads.

Can you replace the tiles?'

'Yes, sir. We'll do it before we leave this evening. Nasty old storm blowing this way, I reckon.' The man nodded at his friend. 'What you think, Silas?'

'Reckon so. Best get these holes fixed right quick then.'

An hour later, Lucas shinned down the ladder and shrugged into his discarded shirt. His skin tingled as he recalled the shock on Demelza's face when she'd spied him unclothed on the roof. He decided not to wash under the pump this time but retreat to the privacy of his own chamber.

He heard the murmur of voices coming from the school room and was tempted to interrupt the children's studies. No — it would be better if he avoided contact with all the family. At the end of the summer he would be gone, and he wished to leave no broken hearts behind him.

Jethro was nowhere to be seen, and the stable boy and newly appointed groom had not yet arrived. He would have to saddle Bruno himself. The walk to the village was no more than a mile, but his gelding needed exercise, so he would ride around the neighbourhood before visiting Tregorran.

After an enjoyable hour, he saw a substantial manor house nestling in a valley. Was this the home of Squire Reynolds? A visit to this gentleman made sense. Reynolds was the magistrate in this area and would surely know if Demelza's fear was correct.

He cantered down the grassy slope looking for a gap in the gorse hedge. Eventually he found a way through the prickly barrier onto the narrow lane which led to the house. He was impressed by the well-manicured park and the weed-free drive; this was obviously a prosperous establishment.

Two gardeners looked up from their tasks and touched their caps as he trotted past. Before he had time to dismount, a smart stable boy appeared from behind the house and the front door opened. A tall gentleman dressed in an old-fashioned frockcoat and knee breeches hurried down the marble steps to greet him.

'Good afternoon, my dear sir. I am Squire Reynolds. How can I be of service?'

Lucas dropped to the ground and tossed his reins to the waiting groom. 'Lucas Fairfield. I am residing with Miss Tregorran for the summer and thought I would pay my respects.'

He nodded and his host reciprocated. Civilities over, the squire beamed and gestured towards Bruno, who was being led away.

'A fine beast you have there, Fairfield. I always admire top-quality horseflesh.' Scarcely pausing for breath, he continued. 'Come along in. I am starved for company presently, as my lady wife is staying with our daughter in Cumbria. Another grandchild is due to arrive soon. Daughters need their mothers on such an occasion, do they not?' Not waiting for a reply, he continued. 'Your horse? Have you had him long?'

'Bruno was with me on the Peninsula . . . '

'My word! I knew it! You have the look of a soldier. You must tell me all about your exploits. I am a dull dog, I can assure you; nothing of any excitement happens in this neighbourhood.'

Lucas followed him in, nodding and smiling as appropriate in the squire's monologue. He was escorted to a book-lined room redolent of tobacco smoke, and where every surface was piled high with a miscellany of papers and books.

'Take a seat, my dear sir. Pray excuse the disarray. I do not allow the parlour maids into my study.'

'Thank you.' Lucas glanced at the nearest sagging armchair, also covered with an assortment of objects. He smiled. 'Shall I put these items elsewhere?'

His genial host smiled and nodded. 'Do that, do that, dear sir. Those items are of no value to me. Toss them aside and sit down. I asked for refreshments to be brought here immediately. Do you know, I saw you turn into my drive and decided at once you looked a likely fellow. I have ordered bread and cheese, meat pasties and whatever else Cook has available in the kitchen.'

Lucas gathered an armful of unwanted books and papers and dropped them on the faded rug. 'Excellent, Squire Reynolds. I am sharp set. I spent the morning scrambling all over the roof of Tregorran House and the last hour or so I have been exploring the countryside.'

'Good, good, I like a fellow who is a good trencher man. Ah! I hear the rattle of crockery.'

There was nowhere to put a tray, as the enormous desk and the two side tables were already in use. Lucas stood up, collected three piles of documents, and dropped them on top of the books he'd already moved. 'There, sir; we now have somewhere to put the food.'

'Well done, indeed, Fairfield. I fear I must do something about the chaos in this room. My good wife is the only person I trust to keep my sanctum in order.'

From the look of the chamber, his wife must have been away for a considerable time, or else was an indifferent housekeeper. A hesitant knock on the door heralded the arrival of the much-anticipated refreshments.

'Come in, damn you. Don't stand dithering outside the door.' The squire's outburst shocked Lucas. The door swung open and two nervous maids sidled in, casting sideways glances at their master. They put the food and drink on the newly cleared space on the desk. Reynolds nodded at the girls but offered no thanks. They curtsied and scuttled off without having uttered a word.

Reynolds gave the impression of being a mild-mannered man, a buffoon almost, but his staff obviously viewed him quite differently. Lucas hid his disquiet under the guise of examining the various dishes and plates. 'This looks quite delicious. Shall I serve myself, sir?'

'Yes, please do so. I can recommend the venison pasty, and you'll find the fruit chutney is the perfect complement.' The squire didn't wait, but began to pile his own plate high.

'I see we have porter, coffee and something that looks like buttermilk,' Lucas said, sniffing the jug suspiciously. 'I shall have coffee; what about you?'

Soon they were both munching contentedly. The meal was excellent, the coffee even better. The voluble Reynolds was quiet whilst he devoured his meal. Lucas took the opportunity to study his surroundings. Was this the room of a disorganised, benign old gentleman, or something else entirely? Beneath the detritus and debris the furniture was polished and dust-free. A quick glance at the walls and ceiling revealed no cobwebs. Surely if no one cleaned in here, the room would have an air of neglect, but this was not apparent. Squire Reynolds didn't look like a man who would wield a duster himself, so someone else must be allowed into this room apart from his missing wife. A clatter of cutlery tossed onto an empty china plate ended his contemplation.

'Excellent repast! Good heavens, man, you've not finished your food. Is it not to your liking?'

'I beg your pardon, I was wool-gathering.' Lucas attacked his meal and smiled around a mouthful of venison pasty. This was enough to satisfy his host.

'I prefer to dine late. Sometimes I don't eat until eight o'clock; therefore I shall finish up the cold cuts and bread whilst you eat.'

After a second serving of coffee and a slice of tasty plum cake, Lucas was replete. 'That was most enjoyable, sir. I take it that you know of my situation, why I am in residence at Tregorran House?'

'Indeed I do, Mr Fairfield. You are a man of means idling the summer away before returning to face his responsibilities. You have moved into Tregorran House in order to assist Miss Tregorran. From what I've heard they have always been a proud family, not used to asking for help from anyone. It would seem the girl has been struggling since her father died last year.' He nodded. 'I should be delighted to offer assistance, financial or any other kind, but she has not applied to me.'

'I am a paying guest, no more, and if my small contribution makes that family's life easier then I too am delighted.' Lucas stiffened. He detected something other than benevolence in the squire's watery blue eyes. Was he imagining it? Did this man not wish him to be involved with Demelza and her family?

'Perhaps, Squire Reynolds, when your wife returns . . . '

'I have no notion when that might be. I don't expect her back until after you depart.'

'Small wonder you are lonely then, sir. I expect your duties keep you busy. Miss Tregoran tells me there are smugglers working in this area?'

'What did Miss Tregorran say?' His tone was sharp.

'She told me there seems to be an arrangement of convenience between those engaged in illegal activities and the revenue men, but I hardly credit it.' Lucas kept his tone light as if he thought the matter amusing.

'Hah! You are right to be sceptical. As you are well aware, sir, I am the magistrate hereabouts. For such a thing to be true, I would have to be involved.'

'As I thought — no more than a young girl's romantic fancies. However, her concern about the arrival of some rough strangers in the village is genuine enough. She fears they might instigate trouble with the locals. I said I could look into the matter.'

'No need to do that, my dear fellow. Leave it to me. I shall make enquiries, and if she is correct then I shall have the men moved on.'

'Thank you, sir. I am glad to leave this in such capable hands.' He brushed the crumbs from his breeches and stood up. 'I thank you for an excellent repast, Squire Reynolds, but I fear I must depart. I've several errands to run in the village before I return home.' He shrugged. 'I'm organising the repairing of the roof and I need more nails and timber to complete the job.'

'A strange way for a house-guest to behave. I thought you purported to be an artist, sir?'

'I dabble, that is all. I much prefer to be busy doing something useful. There are labourers for the other less urgent tasks. Another storm and she will lose several ceilings.'

'Well done, indeed, Mr Fairfield. I am sure your hard work is much appreciated. I do hope you will find time to call in again soon. Kindly convey my best wishes to dear Miss Tregorran. No doubt I shall see you both at church on Sunday.'

They nodded and Lucas strode to the door. For some reason his meal was not sitting comfortably in his stomach. The room had become oppressive — his host less genial. He was glad to step outside and relieved to see a groom waiting with his horse.

He urged Bruno into a canter and was soon back on the downs and heading for the village. He had told the squire he would not investigate the strangers, but he'd lied. There was something havey-cavey going on and he was sure Squire Reynolds was in the thick of it.

*　*　*

Demelza waited in vain for Betty to come to help her downstairs for dinner. The children had been invisible all day. She was decidedly put out, even though she knew the situation was entirely of her own doing. She had even found the pretty blue glass necklace and earbobs that matched her gown.

Even ringing the bell produced no response. Surely the servants were not ignoring her as well? At five o'clock Betty arrived with a tray. 'I reckon you've been a-wondering what's going on, miss. The doctor has took himself to the village and madam had nursery tea with the children.'

The tray was placed on Demelza's lap and she viewed her meal with displeasure. Meat pasty, potatoes and beans would normally have pleased her, but tonight she was too cross to appreciate the appetising aroma. She was tempted to tell the girl to take it away, but that would be impolite and childish. 'Thank you. Could you put it on the table by the window? I'll sit there to eat.'

Although Demelza waited at the window until almost midnight, she didn't see Lucas return. Eventually she disrobed and climbed into bed, thoroughly dispirited. Tomorrow she must apologise again to Lucas for suggesting he fall off the roof. There was no necessity for him to take himself to the village every evening in order to avoid her company.

Her bed was hot, the sheets uncomfortable. She could not settle. Was he back? Dare she go and look? She tossed back the cover and scrambled out of bed. Moments later she was in her bed-robe and hobbling to the door. The hinges squeaked — she froze. Would Serena wake? She breathed again. All was silent.

She hobbled as quietly as she could to the rear of the building, where his rooms were. Her heart thudded. Her hands were clammy. What if he came out and saw her in her night things? Would he think she was checking up on him? Or — even worse — that she was intending to visit him in his bedchamber?

She was about to retreat when she heard the thump of the back door opening and closing. Lucas was home at last. Hastily, she gathered up her skirts and half ran to the safety of her own bedroom. The church clock had struck one o'clock some time ago. Where had her lodger been until so late?

With a heavy heart, she returned to bed. There was one possible explanation for his tardiness. He had been visiting a lady of the night. This was a gentleman's prerogative, of course, and it was no business of hers to pass judgement, but she had thought better of him.

★ ★ ★

Lucas staggered into the kitchen table and cursed loudly. He was in his cups — heaven knew how he'd managed to return from the village without mishap. He'd barely succeeded in staying upright in the saddle; Bruno could have tipped him into the nearest ditch.

His head was pounding and his eyes were blurred; he couldn't remember ever being in such a state before. The local cider had been his undoing.

Blearily, he examined his bruised knuckles. Had he been involved in a brawl as well? He had no recollection of it. He'd lost count of the times the barmaid had refilled his mug. He pushed himself upright and patted his pocket — strange; he still had the coins he'd set out with. He was as drunk as a wheelbarrow but obviously at someone else's expense.

He could scarcely remember his own name, let alone who he'd talked to and what they'd discussed. Maybe tomorrow when he'd had time to sober up he would recall the conversations. He had a rough idea where the door leading into the entrance hall was situated; hopefully he could find his way there without knocking anything over.

Moonlight streamed in the windows either side of the front door, bathing it in eerie white light. He viewed the staircase with horror. The state he was in, he would probably fall and break his neck on the way up. Better to sleep on the floor in the drawing-room. He'd spent the night in far more uncomfortable places in the past. God willing, old Jethro would wake him so he could retire to his own chambers before Demelza or the children came down and discovered him sprawled on the carpet.

Female voices woke him the next morning. His head hurt like the very devil, but that this was no more than he deserved for his overindulgence. He enjoyed a glass of wine like any gentleman but had never been so inebriated before. He was thoroughly ashamed of himself. The girls were coming down to begin their day's work; he had ample time to regain his apartment before he was discovered by anyone else.

He waited until the kitchen door closed behind the maids before slipping out from the drawing-room. With his boots in one hand, he tiptoed like a burglar through the house without being seen. He drew the shutters closed and pulled the curtains. The birds greeting the dawn with their song were almost too much to bear. He groaned and collapsed on his bed. He was asleep seconds later.

7

Demelza slept poorly and woke with gritty eyes and a thumping headache. Betty cheerfully pulled back the curtains and plonked down a tray of warm bread and strawberry conserve.

'The storm never did come, miss. Not like old Jethro to be wrong.'

She yawned. 'I'm glad about that. The workmen will have time to finish the repairs.' Should she ask? Yes — better to know where he was so she could avoid him. 'Is Dr Fairfield on the roof again today?'

'Lawks, miss, not likely. He'd fall to his death, the state he's in.'

'What's wrong with him? Is he unwell?'

'Nothing a good sleep won't cure, miss. Came home last night in a sorry way. Bill, that new groom, was telling Jethro — the lads down the village gave him a deal too much cider.'

Demelza's heart skipped. 'They got him drunk? Poor man, that cider is extremely potent. Small wonder he was out so late.' She wished her words unsaid. Now Betty would know she had waited up. 'I was woken by him stumbling about downstairs and thought he had tripped over in the dark.'

Betty laughed. 'Reckon he did that, miss. I've had a look in his room and he's snoring like a hog. Best leave him. He'll have a powerful bad head when he does wake, I can tell you.'

'Serves him right for his overindulgence; I doubt he'll make the same mistake again.' What was she thinking of? She should not be discussing Lucas with her maid. 'I have no further need of your services at present, Betty. Thank you for bringing up my breakfast.'

She ate her meal with relish. Her appetite had returned. She was glad it had only been strong cider that had kept him out — far better than the other. Her shrewish behaviour had been forgiven, at least, by her staff. The breakfast was Molly's way of making peace.

Her foot was sufficiently recovered to allow her to put on stockings and boots. She would not lie about all day doing nothing, but go down to the village. There was bound to be an errand or two Martha or Molly wanted fulfilling. Her lips twitched. Then she would call in and see Mrs Newlyn at The Green Man for refreshments before walking back. If she should hear about Lucas's exploits then so much the better.

Heavy grey clouds were blotting out the sunshine. Maybe there would be another storm after all. She could hardly walk to the village in the rain. Demelza went to the school room to speak to her siblings and her friend and was greeted by cries of delight from the children and a smile from Martha.

'Good morning, everyone. I'm walking down to the village this morning as my foot is no longer sore. Is there anything you would like me to purchase for you, Martha? I believe Miss Percy will have received that delivery of haberdashery by now.'

'We definitely need more thread to complete our needlework, my dear. And I am in desperate need of a hatpin or two. With this stormy weather, I fear I could lose my bonnet next time I go outside.'

'Children? I believe I can spare a penny or two, if you have any requests.'

She departed a few minutes later, promising to return with barley sugar twists for the boys and a new paintbrush for Serena. Her foot was more painful than she'd anticipated, but she was determined to make the journey to the village however much it complained.

Halfway there she regretted her decision. Her foot was throbbing. She was almost certain one of the sutures had come undone, because her foot was sliding unpleasantly inside her boot, which could only indicate the presence of blood. She sank to the grass, clutching her basket and ruing her curiosity. She hated to disappoint the children, but it would be folly to continue. However, the prospect of hobbling back up the steep incline did not appeal.

She had been all too ready to criticise Lucas, even though his inebriation had not been entirely his fault. The village men were infamous for plying an unwary visitor with the local brew. Such a pastime was relatively harmless and caused a great deal of merriment for the onlookers. The folk down there had little enough to laugh about at the moment.

There was no choice; she would have to make her own way back to the house and ask Lucas to attend to her foot. Despite her discomfort she smiled — perhaps it might be better to leave him to sleep.

'What the hell are you doing down here? You have the sense of a pea goose, my girl. Didn't I tell you stay off that foot for three days at least?'

'Good heavens! How did you get here?'

Lucas shook his head and dropped down beside her. 'I was at my ablutions when you went up to the school room.' He grinned and reached out to push an errant strand of hair from her face. 'You have a wonderfully clear voice, my dear.'

'Are you saying that I am overly loud, sir? I was told you wouldn't be up until noon.' She frowned. 'I must say you don't look as if you even have a headache. I was reliably informed that you — '

'What I do or don't do, my girl, is no business of yours. Now, up you come. I suppose I'll have to carry you back to the house.' Without further ado, he pushed his arms under her recumbent form and straightened. 'This is becoming a habit, Miss Tregorran. In my debilitated state it will serve you right if I drop you.'

She glared at him. 'Put me down at once. I have not asked for your assistance and I can assure you I'm quite capable of walking back to the house.'

'Hopping back, perhaps — but, my dear girl, you have to admit you're unable to walk.'

He was quite correct. It galled her to admit it, but she would have been in a sorry state indeed without his timely appearance. 'Yes, Dr Fairfield, you are, as always, perfectly right. It must be wonderful to be such a fount of wisdom.'

He tightened his grip and shook her gently. 'Baggage! Tell me, what possessed you to set off for the village?'

'Martha needed some sewing thread and I promised the children some treats.'

'Fustian, my girl, and you know it. You were heading for The Green Man to quiz Mrs Newlyn about my exploits last night.' He stopped and dropped her none too kindly on the grass. 'Sit there and I shall tell you what you want to know.'

Her face was scorching. He was right to be cross with her. Dare she glance up? No, better to keep her eyes averted until he'd completed his tale.

'I met up with our workmen and they suggested I try the local brew.'

Forgetting her hesitation, she looked up. 'Is that all? That's hardly worth the telling.'

He scooped her into the air once more. 'Exactly so, my dear. I remember nothing about the evening apart from discovering the potency of Cornish cider.'

He was a decidedly annoying gentleman, but she could hardly say so whilst he was striding so heroically up the steep incline with her in his arms. She relaxed into his hold, rather enjoying the sensation of being clasped close to a gentleman's chest. Demelza had been holding her breath, not wishing to inhale fumes from last night's cider, but he smelled no different — lemon soap, leather, and a salty tang she guessed was perspiration.

'If you would care to put me down, I'm quite capable of hopping the rest of the way.' He ignored her request and continued to march towards the house. She tried again. 'Dr Fairfield, what will the staff think if they see me like this? I have no wish to be the subject of their gossip.'

This got his attention. In one smooth motion he slipped her from horizontal to upright, but his arm remained firmly about her waist. 'Very well, my dear, I will allow you to hobble the rest of the way. Let me take your weight — don't try and use the injured foot.'

'Thank you. I believe I must apologise for my intemperate outburst yesterday. I'm not usually like that; I'm normally a quiet and gently spoken young lady.'

His snort of derision made an answer unnecessary.

She hung back, forcing him to halt. 'Dr Fairfield, am I to take it that you don't consider me demure and well-mannered?'

'My dear child, you are as volatile as the ocean.'

She was about to argue the point but was cut short by the heavens opening. She didn't protest when he tightened his hold and ran headlong for the shelter of the house. Even so, they were drenched when they entered the vestibule. His soft white shirt clung damply to his chest and her flimsy muslin gown left little to the imagination.

Embarrassment made her unnecessarily curt. 'Thank you, sir, I can manage the stairs on my own.'

Yet again he ignored her and half carried her straight up to her apartment. He shouldered his way in and released her unceremoniously on the chaise longue. 'I'll fetch your maid servant to assist you,' he said. 'I'll return with my medical bag in fifteen minutes.'

Allowing her no time to disagree, he vanished. Her foot was throbbing painfully and she was decidedly uncomfortable in a wet gown and stockings.

She removed her bonnet, which was drooping sadly. Botheration! The pretty green ribbon was quite ruined. She scrubbed at her wet cheeks and was horrified to see her hand come away green. What must he have thought? Quite forgetting her injury, she jumped up to inspect her face in the glass. As her weight transferred to her foot she cried out and toppled forward. Unable to stop herself, she fell and her forehead stuck the corner of the mantle-shelf with a sickening thud. Her world went black.

★ ★ ★

Lucas turned to go downstairs to the kitchen to collect what he needed and direct Betty to Demelza's parlour. He was three strides from her door when something heavy crashed to the floor. He was back inside in seconds. She was on the carpet, one hand outstretched as if in supplication.

'Sweetheart, what's wrong? Did you

trip?' He dropped to his knees and gently touched her shoulder. She remained inert. He rolled her over and his throat constricted. The ominous blue dent on her forehead told him what had occurred. She was unconscious, having hit her head on something as she fell.

Her limbs were obviously intact, but a head injury was far more serious, especially when the patient remained unconscious for any length of time.

'Miss Tregorran, can you hear me? You have banged your head. I'm going to carry you to your bedchamber.' He needed urgent assistance. Not only was there the damage to her forehead; there was also the matter of her foot to be dealt with. He walked to the door with her in his arms and bellowed down the corridor.

Mrs Smith appeared from the school room stairs. 'Oh dear! Has dear Demelza met with another accident?'

'She appears to have fallen and struck her head. I can't deal with this until someone removes her wet clothes. She's already chilled to the marrow.'

'Take her into her bedchamber, Dr Fairfield. I shall take care of her. I'll need the assistance of Betty . . . '

'I'll fetch her. I'm going to need hot water and clean cloths from the kitchen. I fear she has opened the wound on her foot as well.' He turned and carried his precious burden into the bedroom, placing her carefully on the coverlet. Her head flopped on the pillow and her eyes remained closed. She had already been unconscious for more than five minutes. Not a good sign.

By the time he'd assembled what he needed and raced upstairs, his patient had been re-clothed in a voluminous nightgown. Betty was holding a cold compress to Demelza's forehead whilst the other girl, Josie, pressed a folded cloth to the foot wound.

'Excellent,' Lucas said. 'As I thought, Mrs Smith, I shall need to suture Miss Tregorran's foot, but that must wait until I've examined her head injury. Has she shown any sign of waking?'

'No, she has not. She's rather too pale for my liking and her breathing's shallow. Is this a bad sign, Doctor?'

Lucas pushed down his fear. There was no point in alarming this good lady or the children. 'Let me check.' He pressed his finger into the space at the apex of her jaw and her neck. 'Her pulse is regular and reasonably strong; that's reassuring.' Next he carefully ran his fingertips across her skull, checking for any irregularities that might indicate a fracture. 'As far as I can judge, Mrs Smith, the injury is not as bad as we feared. I can find no evidence of a fracture to the skull. The cold compresses are an excellent idea — if you would continue with those, I'll take care of the foot.'

'There's a deal of blood coming from it, sir, even though I'm holding the cloth tight,' Josie told him.

'I'll deal with that now I'm sure she's in no danger from her head injury.' He gathered the items he needed and positioned himself on the end of the bed. As he thought, her efforts to walk into the village had torn a couple of stitches. With expert fingers, he repaired the wound and carefully wrapped a clean strip of linen around his work. He was about to stand up when the bedchamber door flew open and the children burst in.

Serena was clinging to her brothers, barely able to restrain them as they were so eager to reach their sister.

'Why's Melza asleep? It's not bed-time,' Tom said as he struggled to remove his hand from Serena's grip.

Mrs Smith moved swiftly to their side. 'Your sister fell and knocked herself out, children. She will be better presently. Now, did I give you permission to leave your desks?'

The boys quietened and all three shook their heads. 'No, Mrs Smith, you didn't.'

'Then we shall return upstairs and continue with our lessons.' She nodded at Josie. 'Please ask Molly for lemonade and plum cake and bring it immediately to the school room.' She bundled the children from the room and Lucas heard them chatting happily as if nothing untoward had occurred. He prayed his assessment of the situation was correct and that his patient suffered no worse than a mild concussion. He would not leave her side until she was fully conscious once more.

★ ★ ★

Someone was calling her name. Whoever it was, was most insistent that she wake up and answer them. Reluctantly, Demelza dragged herself from the comfort of the darkness and slowly opened her eyes.

'At last, Miss Tregorran. You have taken an unconscionable time to recover. How is your head?'

'It hurts abominably and so does my foot. What are you doing in my bedchamber, sir?'

Lucas smiled. 'I am your physician, my dear. It's my job to remain at your bedside until you are well enough to be left with someone else. Don't you remember falling?'

She frowned and wished she hadn't. Heavens above! 'My face! I got up to investigate.'

'Betty has removed all traces of green, my love. I now understand your urgent desire to purchase fresh ribbons for your bonnet.' He chuckled; the sound raised her spirits. 'I shall ensure the next one you have is of better quality.'

She closed her eyes. Why should he wish to buy her a new bonnet? One minute he was calling her a child, the next using inappropriate endearments. She was confused by his behaviour but couldn't think about it at the moment.

'Sleep, my dear. You will feel more the thing when you next wake.'

She was almost sure his lips brushed her forehead before he left,, but that might have been her imagination playing tricks on her. She had only herself to blame for her predicament. Curiosity was said to kill the cat and she had certainly paid the price for her desire to garner gossip about her house-guest. In future she wouldn't attempt to interfere in business that did not concern her. If Lucas wished to drink himself insensible on the potent local brew, this was entirely his concern.

A roll of distant thunder roused her. Thank God she no longer had to worry about the holes in the roof. Lightning lit up the room and a gust of wind slammed her door. She shivered. These sudden summer storms were dangerous for those unfortunate to be caught out at sea. The ferocity of the winds and power of the waves could prove fatal to the unwary.

8

Downstairs in the drawing-room, Lucas turned to Mrs Smith, who was fidgeting behind him. 'I'm sure there's nothing to worry about, ma'am. The roof is sound. The storm sounds far worse than it actually is.' This was less than the truth, but he could hardly tell Demelza's companion he shared her disquiet.

'I do hope so, Dr Fairfield. I can't remember having heard the wind howl so loudly and I have been living in Cornwall this past year. I do declare, it reminds me of a beast in torment.'

Something heavy crashed into the wall outside and the slice of plum cake he was about to eat shot off his plate. He swore. 'I beg your pardon, Mrs Smith. Barrack room manners.' He collected the errant morsel and hastily put both plate and cake on a nearby table. 'I'd better go outside and investigate. Perhaps it might be wise if you checked on the children and Miss Tregorran. I believe Serena can be frightened by thunder.'

'I shall do so at once; thank you for reminding me.' She bustled out and Lucas followed her. He needed to put on his riding coat before venturing outside.

As he passed Demelza's apartment he heard movement inside. She shouldn't be out of bed; even a mild concussion required several days' rest. He knocked on the parlour door and Betty opened it.

'Lawks, sir, a right old storm we're having tonight. The mistress is fast asleep; I'm just having a bit of a tidy round. I'll be sleeping on the truckle-bed in the dressing room tonight, like you instructed.'

'That's good news, Betty. I'm going outside to check everything's secure. I shall call in on the patient before I retire.'

He met Mrs Smith as she retreated

from the boys' bedchamber. 'All three of them are sleeping soundly, Dr Fairfield. It's past nine o'clock, so I shall retire. Please don't hesitate to call if either the children or Demelza have need of me.'

'Thank you, ma'am, but I doubt Miss Tregorran will require your services tonight.'

Although the wind was fierce and the rain torrential, the night wasn't particularly cold, so he decided he would be better off in shirt sleeves and breeches; he would get drenched, but a bit of rain never hurt anyone.

Jethro and Molly had returned to their cottage and only the scullery maid was in the kitchen, scrubbing the table. She bobbed a curtsy but kept her eyes lowered and continued with her task.

'I shall be out some time,' Lucas told her. 'Leave the back door unlocked for me. I'll take care of it when I come in.'

There was little point in taking a lantern, since it would blow out immediately. He unlatched the door.

147

His arm was almost wrenched from its socket as the wind attempted to snatch it from him. Good grief! He didn't envy any ships trying to get into the harbour in such foul weather. He leaned hard against the wood and forced the door closed, then dropped the latch home. He could barely keep his feet; the wind tore around the house and seemed determined to carry away anyone unwise enough to venture out. Several pieces of wood flew past his head, then a heavy object caught him on the shoulder, sending him crashing into the wall.

His mission was foolhardy. He was likely to end up with a concussion of his own if he wasn't careful. He was now at the front of the house, facing the cliffs. Sheet lightning lit the area and by this strange light he saw half a dozen figures manhandling an object that looked like a rowing boat of some sort, down the cliff path. He shook his head and screwed up his eyes to peer through the rain. Surely his imagination was playing tricks on him.

Who the hell would be foolish enough to come out on such a night? No — those were definitely oars being hefted by a couple of the men. He cursed as he understood the significance of their presence. They could only be there for one reason. There must be a vessel heading for the rocks, and these villains were intending to plunder the ship and possibly murder the unfortunate passengers.

*　*　*

The shutter banged for the fourth time. Demelza sighed. She doubted she would get any sleep even if she did somehow hop to the window and fasten the wretched thing. There was less thunder than last time, but far more lightning. Good. This must mean the storm was not directly above the house.

Lucas had gone outside a few minutes ago. She struggled out of bed, glad the nausea and sickening headache had subsided. Her injured foot was well padded with a clean bandage. If she kept her weight on her heel, it would be perfectly possible to reach the window without mishap.

The frequent flashes of white light from outside meant she could see without rekindling a candle. On reaching the offending shutter, she paused to gaze out across the grass to the cliffs. Her fingers gripped the curtain. She swayed. What was Lucas doing at the cliff edge? He could be swept away by the rain and wind. He must be mad to wish to view the sea on a night like this.

She could not bear it if anything happened to him. She swallowed her tears and reached out to close the shutter. What was wrong? Lucas hadn't attempted to descend the dangerous path to the beach, but was racing for the house as if his very life depended on it. There was only one reason she could think of to promote such a reaction — a ship had foundered on the rocks in Tregorran Bay.

However bad her foot, she must throw on some clothes and organise her staff to take care of any sailors or passengers rescued from the wreck. As she was struggling into her gown, she heard the brass bell ringing loudly. This would alert Jethro and the recently employed outdoor men who were living above the stable.

Her dressing-room door flew open and Betty appeared more or less correctly dressed. 'Lawks, miss, you shouldn't be out of bed. Here, let me help. I reckon Josie will go downstairs with Mrs Smith. It's a wreck. God help those aboard the vessel.'

'Amen to that, Betty. I shall remain upstairs and collect blankets and bed linen for the survivors. You and Josie must prepare the two spare bedchambers.'

'There's plenty of room on the top floor, miss, what with the children sleeping down here. Shall we make up some beds there?'

'Yes, a good idea. There, I'm ready. I shall remain without stockings and slippers, but as I'm not intending to go downstairs, I should be perfectly safe.' Leaning heavily on Betty's arm, Demelza hobbled to the door that led into the wide passageway. She came face-to-face with Lucas.

'Good heavens!' she exclaimed. 'You're quite soaked.'

'How observant of you, my dear. And you, I note, are fully dressed and out of bed.'

'I'm feeling perfectly well, apart from my foot. Is it a wreck? What kind of ship is it?'

His smile slipped. 'A small ship — a trading vessel — hopefully without too many souls aboard.' He glanced over her shoulder as if checking that Betty had gone. 'I was only alerted to the disaster by the sight of half a dozen men heading for the path with a boat on their shoulders. I fear their purpose is not to offer assistance but to steal any cargo they can lay their hands on.'

'I knew it. I told you about the ruffians who moved into that derelict cottage in the village. I'm certain it will be them, and a few of the village men with nothing further to lose.'

'I came to tell you I'm taking your men to the beach to see if we can protect the sailors. Jethro is collecting rope, cudgels and any other items that might be of use. I'm going to take my pistols.'

'Be careful, sir. These are desperate men. Have you sent word to the village?'

'Yes of course I have; the stable boy's already on his way. Do you think the villagers will turn out?'

'Not all of them. I doubt Young Johnny or his gang will help. Do you think Squire Reynolds must be told as well?' She was surprised to see him frown.

'I don't think that particular gentleman will be in any hurry to offer his assistance. I didn't get the opportunity to tell you of my visit to his house. I can't delay any longer; I shall explain everything to you when this is done.'

★ ★ ★

This time Lucas shrugged on his riding coat. There was little point in taking his pistols if the powder was allowed to become wet. He deftly loaded each one, then dropped patches, powder and shot into one of the deep pockets in his coat; the guns followed.

The front door was unbolted and he hurtled out that way. He was greeted by a circle of men. Jethro was their spokesman; the old man had to shout in order to make himself heard.

'Right you are, sir, we're a-ready to tackle them waves. Plenty of stout rope as well. Between us I reckon we can save a few of them poor sailors. You'll be a swimmer, then?'

'I am, yes.' Good grief, they expected him to swim out to the vessel! He swallowed his fear. 'Jethro, does everyone understand the danger? Those men are down before us and won't take kindly to our interference.'

One of the men pointed to the cudgel he had leaning against his shoulder. 'We knows how to handle the likes of them. Don't want them sort in our village giving us a bad name.'

'Good, so let's get on with it. The ship will be aground on the rocks by now. The sooner we get to the beach the better.' Holding his coat tight around him, Lucas put his head down and raced for the cliff edge. He paused to take stock of the situation. The men he'd spied earlier were nowhere to be seen. However, the doomed ship was exactly where he'd expected — on the rocks. Her prow was visible above the crashing waves, and even from this distance he could see a group of men clustered at the rail, clinging on for dear life.

Without waiting to check that his motley crew were following, he plunged through the gorse bushes. His headlong rush sent his feet from under him. Straightening his legs, he careened down the narrow path, thanking God he'd had the foresight to envelop himself in his thick coat.

Where the hell were the missing men? As he tumbled to the sand, he remembered Demelza telling him the beach all but vanished beneath the incoming tide. Too late to repine. He was a strong swimmer, unlike many sailors who preferred a quick drowning if they were unfortunate enough to go overboard.

He arrived pell-mell at the bottom of the path, relieved his feet hit sand and not water. From the amount of noise and cursing coming from above, the four men had adopted his method of descent. There was no need to be furtive in their approach; the beach was deserted.

He flicked open his spyglass and turned it towards the ship. Now he knew where his quarries were — they were rowing towards the wreck. Had he misjudged their intent? Were they in fact braving the fearsome waves in order to rescue the crew?

'Them varmints! They'll do for them poor lads if we don't stop them,' Jethro shouted in his ear.

'How can you be sure they're up to no good? Couldn't they be effecting a rescue?'

'Ain't likely, sir. See the boat? It's not from around these parts. Young Johnny and his crew don't have anything so fine. No, them lot's after the cargo. I reckon there's something valuable aboard.'

Lucas stripped off his coat and removed his boots. 'It can be no more than one hundred yards to the rocks. Even in this sea I should be able to make it.'

'They'll have a rope ready, sir, and it'll be easier coming back with the tide. Me and the boys just have to make it fast, and then the crew can get to the beach.'

'Jethro, I've pistols in that pocket.

Don't hesitate to use them if need be.'

The waves curled and broke at head height, making it nigh on impossible to wade through the breakers. Lucas prayed he hadn't overestimated his aquatic ability. All he had to do was swim out, somehow climb aboard, and collect a rope from the men.

The icy waves almost engulfed him. He staggered and fell to his knees. The water closed over his head and he tumbled over and over, not knowing which way was up. His feet touched the bottom and he kicked off forcefully, shooting to the surface. His eyes stung and he was gasping for breath, but he was alive.

From the depths of a wave, the distance to the ship seemed all but impossible. He doubted he would reach the stranded men. However, things were easier now he was swimming. As he ploughed through the water, he tried to keep the bobbing lanterns on the stricken ship ahead of him.

The wreckers in their longboat were

heading for the hold, not the crew. Whatever was being transported must be valuable indeed. The ship could break up at any time and clambering aboard at the stern was going to be hazardous.

Lucas was sure he was getting no closer; that he was barely holding his position. The tide was coming in and he was swimming against the current. Then he heard voices, men shouting — he was almost there. With renewed energy, he swam towards the sound.

An enormous wave tossed him forward and he crashed into the hull. He couldn't fail now; he was too close to success. His fingers clawed at the wood, trying to find purchase. Thank the good Lord! His hands became entangled in a mesh of rope and he was being dragged upwards, banging and crashing painfully against the side, but he barely felt it.

'You've done it! Well done, sir.' Rough hands thumped him on the back, clearing his lungs of seawater. 'Give the gentleman the rope, Freddie. We ain't got much time.'

'Has the boat reached you?' Lucas's voice was barely above a whisper. It hurt to swallow.

'Never you mind about that, sir. Them varmints are welcome to try for my cargo, but I reckon they'll perish in the attempt.' The speaker was obviously the captain, although Lucas couldn't tell from his appearance. He was as wet and dishevelled as his men.

Lucas was too exhausted to enquire further. The thought of making the return journey appalled him; he would need to rest for a minute and recoup his strength before attempting it. He flopped onto the heaving deck and closed his eyes. Far too soon, he was shaken awake.

'Right then, sir, you need to get this rope back to the beach smartish. You get your men to tie it and then we can haul ourselves to safety.'

Lucas slithered to the edge of the

deck, one end of the rope secured to his waist.

'The tide's with you. I reckon you'll find it a sight easier getting back.'

Lucas threw himself headfirst from the deck. This time the water seemed less cold and he more buoyant. The captain had been right — all he had to do was keep his head above the water and kick. Only minutes after launching himself from the ship, his feet touched sand. He was dragged the last few yards by two of the men and they untangled the rope from his middle. He doubled up, retching and coughing, scarcely able to believe he'd accomplished his mission. Somebody draped his coat around his shoulders and pushed his boots into his limp fingers.

He had time to gather his wits whilst his men looped the rope around a convenient boulder. He was upright, boots safely on this feet, as the first of the sailors arrived, quickly followed by the others. The rain showed no sign of easing, nor the wind of abating.

'Can you see the longboat, Jethro? Have those men gone aboard?' he asked.

'Don't rightly know, sir, but that's not our problem. We needs to get off this here beach before we're trapped. Tide's coming in right fast.'

Only then did Lucas realise the sea was almost upon them. 'Captain, are all your men safely ashore?'

'Indeed they are, thanks to you, sir.'

'Then follow me. This path leads up to Tregorran House, where preparations are being made to receive you. Untie the rope, John, before you leave the beach.' Immediately the waves swallowed it.

John pointed at the ship. Lucas saw a smuggler clinging to the wreckage. He was scrambling towards the bows in order to grab the rope, but he was too late.

'I never saw him there, sir, or I'd not have let the rope go.'

'It's not your fault, John. There's nothing we can do for the wretched man. I wish it were otherwise.' Lucas turned away, his heart heavy, and began the arduous climb up the steep cliff path.

The ascent took longer than he'd expected. Several times he was forced to grab the prickly bushes to steady himself. He tumbled onto the grass with a sigh of relief, rolling sideways in order to allow the other men to reach safety.

Tregorran was ablaze, all the downstairs rooms lit with welcoming candlelight. Demelza had been busy in his absence. He was about to lead the exhausted group towards the house, when someone grabbed his elbow. He looked round to see the captain behind him.

'Might I have a word with you in private, sir?'

'Not here, Captain. I can scarcely make out what you're saying above the wind. As soon as we're inside I'll take you somewhere quiet where we can talk.'

'I want to give you this. I've brought it from France and was supposed to give it to a military gentleman in Plymouth. We got caught in the storm and blown onto your rocks. I reckon you'll do instead.'

'But I'm not anything to do with the military.'

'One of your men told me you was on the Peninsula. Makes you a soldier in my book,' the man shouted.

Before Lucas could protest, an oilskin-wrapped parcel was slipped into his pocket. The captain rejoined his men as if he'd not just handed over state secrets to a complete stranger. Lucas cursed under his breath. The last thing he wanted was to be in possession of a document belonging to the government.

A sudden shout made him look round. The last of the sailors appeared from the path. He was pointing to the beach. Lucas turned and, with the other men, staggered back against the wind and rain to see what the fuss was about.

He stopped and flipped open his spyglass. The ship was no longer there, and neither were the looters or their longboat. The captain had spoken truly about the risks involved in trying to empty the hold of a sinking ship. There was nothing Lucas could do for those men. He sent up a quick prayer to the Almighty that somehow they might find their way ashore. They were villains, but they didn't deserve to die.

9

'Martha, why are they taking so long? It must be more than an hour since Dr Fairfield and the men went down to the beach.'

'Demelza, my dear, he could hardly effect a rescue in less time than this. Come away from the window and drink your tea. You'll be busy enough when he returns with the crew.'

'I can't imagine why no one has turned up from the village to assist. The stable boy returned some time ago, didn't he?'

Betty, who was industriously stitching a large rent in a sheet, looked up. 'The lad reckons they ain't coming. They've been got at by them foreigners.'

'Oh dear! I knew those incomers were going to be trouble. I suppose if Squire Reynolds hadn't turned a blind eye to the smuggling this would never have happened.' She dropped the curtain and hopped back to her chair. She was too anxious to settle; she could hardly tell Martha how much the safety of their house-guest meant to her.

'I must admit, my dear, that I do find it most reprehensible of the magistrate to be actively involved in such a dishonest pastime.'

'Good heavens, Martha, Mr Reynolds is hardly involved. He, like Papa, accepts the local men would be unable to manage without the income they receive from contraband.' She glanced across at Betty, who was studiously ignoring the improper turn of the conversation. The tea was tepid and she replaced the cup with a sigh. She was relieved when the tedium was broken by a rapid knock on the door. Betty dropped her sewing and hurried over to open it.

Whoever was there didn't wish to come in. Betty stepped outside and pulled the door shut. How strange!

Martha immediately got up, her mouth pursed.

'This will not do, my dear. It's not for a servant to decide who enters your parlour.' Her friend marched purposefully across the room and pulled open the door. 'Good gracious, where ever has the girl got to?'

'Please would you go downstairs and see what's going on. I'm afraid my head and my foot are preventing me from finding out for myself.'

'Remain where you are, my dear. I shall be back in no time.'

The clock struck twice. She yawned. This was going to be a long night for all of them. Demelza pushed herself upright and, using the furniture to take her weight, she edged her way across to the window. The shutter had been left open on one side, which allowed her to see across the grass to the cliff edge.

At last! There was movement at the top of the path — someone was emerging. Her heart skipped when she recognised the figure. It could only be

Lucas; he was so much taller than everyone else. As she watched, several more figures stumbled through the bushes until there was a small crowd gathered on the grass.

Why was he dallying there? The rain was as heavy as ever — surely he must wish to get in the warm. She pressed her nose to the glass. One of the men had waylaid Lucas and was giving him something. No doubt it was recompense for his bravery.

Jethro was easy to distinguish from the group, his ungainly gait quite clear even in the intermittent glow of lightning. He was leading the rescued men towards the house. Why hadn't someone from downstairs gone out to meet them?

She was about to turn away, when the entire group made their way back to the gorse bushes. She shuddered. She could think of only one thing that would draw them there — the ship had sunk, taking anyone left on board with her.

Where was Martha? She couldn't dither about in her chambers; maybe she would bump her way down the stairs on her backside and find out what was going on. With luck, she would have completed this ungainly procedure before Lucas and his party arrived at the house.

The sound of angry voices echoed up the stairway and she didn't recognise any of them. Should she go, or wait until Lucas returned to deal with the matter? No — she was mistress in this house, and whatever the problem, she should be the one to deal with it.

She slithered down the stairs and arrived in an ungainly heap on the polished floor of the vestibule. Nothing, apart from her dignity, had been damaged by her rapid descent. Using the banister to heave herself up would be easiest. Unfortunately her skirts had become entangled beneath her, and far more of her bare legs were showing than was proper.

The argument in the kitchen was

becoming more heated. Was that Molly shouting? With her skirts returned to their correct position, Demelza was ready to intervene. But before she could take more than one shuffling step, there was a crash of falling furniture, rapidly followed by breaking crockery. Ignoring the pain in her foot, she hurried to the door and threw it open, expecting to see grown men engaged in fisticuffs. 'Stop that at once. How dare you behave in such a way in my house?'

Instead of men, there were two boys fighting with Jimmy. What was her stable lad doing inside? And who were these wretched boys? Three chairs were tipped over and several plates from the dresser had smashed on the flagstones.

At the sound of her voice, all three looked round and then scrambled to their feet. One of the unknown boys had a bloody nose and a black eye; the other appeared undamaged. Jimmy touched his forelock and squared his shoulders but seemed remarkably unrepentant.

'I'm waiting. What's going on? Who are these boys and why are they in my kitchen?'

Molly emerged from the pantry with a broom in her hand. 'I was going to stop them with this here broom, Miss Tregorran. I've never seen the like. Jimmy was sitting quiet-like, at the table drying off after returning from the village, when these two knocked at the door. Jimmy opened the door, and before we knew it they were brawling all over the kitchen.'

Josie approached the strange youths and made shooing gestures. 'Be off with you, you varmints. Get outside where you belong.'

The two miscreants seemed more than ready to make their escape. 'Jimmy, stand at the door. I wish to question the boys before they are allowed to leave.'

* * *

172

Lucas was puzzled by the lack of activity in the house. Every room was lit with a dozen candles, so they were expected. Why was nobody out here? Maybe the staff were in the kitchen preparing refreshments for them all? He hoped so; God knew they all needed it. 'Come inside, men; there'll be hot drinks and dry blankets for all of you.'

'We'll not go in the front, sir. The likes of us go round the back,' the captain said.

'Right — take them to the kitchen, Jethro.'

The front door was unbolted and he shoved it open. The drawing-room fire was well alight and a stack of blankets and towels stood waiting. These would not be needed, as there were no passengers to take care of. No doubt there would be others in the servants' quarters for the half-a-dozen men he'd rescued.

He stood dripping in the vestibule, not sure if he had the energy to investigate. Demelza would want to know what happened; he would change into something dry and seek her out.

Lucas had taken no more than two steps when he heard her voice. What the devil was she doing down here? Fatigue forgotten, he headed for the kitchen. He flung open the door and stopped in amazement. 'What's going on here?'

The room was in disarray, chairs and broken crockery everywhere. The stable boy was attempting to keep two unkempt youths from departing. On hearing his voice, one of them looked over his shoulder before charging for the door and sending Jimmy flying. The taller of the two, who looked vaguely familiar, snatched open the door and prepared to flee. The boys came face-to-face with Bill and the rest of the men.

'Hang on to those two, Bill,' Lucas said. 'I'll interrogate them tomorrow. Shove them in the woodshed for the remainder of the night.'

'Right you are, sir. They'll come to no harm in there,' Bill replied. He grabbed the nearest miscreant by the collar and Silas apprehended the other boy. They were dragged away, kicking and swearing, into the night. Lucas frowned. That boy he'd recognised — he was the groom who'd taken Bruno when he'd visited the squire. He shook his head. No point in trying to work this out tonight; he was too tired. He would get to the bottom of this in the morning.

'Dr Fairfield, I'm so glad to see you back safe and well.' Demelza's smile warmed him to his very heart. 'Come along in, gentlemen. Molly will serve you hot soup and sweet tea. I shall — '

Lucas interrupted her quickly. The men were obviously uncomfortable in the company of a lady. 'Miss Tregorran, allow me to escort you upstairs. I wish to get out of my wet garments and then I must speak to you.'

She opened her mouth to argue, but seeing his expression thought better of it. 'Molly, I shall leave you and the girls to cater for our guests. I don't expect any of you to be up at your usual time.

175

We shall all need our rest after so much excitement.'

The captain touched his forelock. 'Thank you kindly, miss. Me and my men are right grateful for your hospitality.' He straightened and nodded at Lucas. 'I've not introduced myself, sir. Captain Jack Benbow, at your service.'

'Lucas Fairfield. Delighted to meet you, Captain Benbow. Now, if you'll excuse me, I must go to my apartment. I'll see you tomorrow.' He guided Demelza from the room, concerned that she was leaning so much of her weight on his arm. 'Your foot is painful, my dear?'

She nodded and smiled ruefully. 'I shouldn't have come down. There's no need for you to lecture me, sir. There was such a ruckus going on in the kitchen, I could hardly remain aloof.'

Mrs Smith joined them in the vestibule. 'Do you need my assistance, Demelza, my dear?'

'No, thank you, Martha. You must retire. We've all been up far too long already. I'm surprised the children haven't been disturbed by the noise and come down to join us.'

'I expect they'll be up bright and early as always. Never fear, my dear girl; I shall be on duty to supervise them. You must remain in bed. Good heavens, child; scarcely five hours ago you were all but unconscious.'

They embraced fondly and Demelza's kind companion hurried up the stairs. Without waiting for permission, Lucas put his arm around her, belatedly realising she would be quite damp by the time he'd escorted her to her room.

'I apologise, sweetheart, for soaking you; but as your physician, I can't allow you to remain on your feet a moment longer than necessary.'

★　★　★

'No matter, I shan't argue this time. I'm feeling rather peculiar and will be profoundly grateful to get to bed.' Demelza's face burned. How could she have been so indelicate as to mention getting into her bed? 'I beg your pardon . . . '

Lucas's laughter reassured her he wasn't shocked by her immodesty. 'Hush, my dear. I believe we know each other too well to worry about formality.'

He hesitated at the door to her parlour, his breathing ragged. How could she have allowed him to help her when he was so exhausted? 'Thank you, Dr Fairfield. I can manage perfectly well from here. Please take care of yourself. Whatever you have to tell me can wait until we are both feeling more the thing.'

He pushed himself from the door-jamb and marched firmly across the room, and without pause straight into her bedchamber. He dropped her unceremoniously on the bed. 'There you are. You will have to manage alone. I'll take your advice, sweetheart, and turn in myself. I'm too tired to even to wash the salt from my face.'

'Make sure you have hot water

brought up tomorrow morning so you can take a bath. Good night. Go to your rooms before you fall asleep on my floor.'

He grinned and with a casual wave left her to her own devices. She hadn't been exaggerating when she'd told him she felt a trifle odd. Her head was spinning unpleasantly and she was not sure she could manage to remove her clothes without assistance. If they were not so damp from being in close contact with Lucas she would sleep as she was.

She closed her eyes and drew several steadying breaths, then began the difficult process of removing her gown and underpinnings. For some reason her limbs refused to answer commands. She flopped onto her pillows, intending to close her eyes for a moment, but blackness once more overwhelmed her.

*　*　*

Lucas staggered like a drunken sailor down the passageway, not sure he would reach his apartment without collapsing. Thank God there were candles burning; his hands were shaking too much to use the tinderbox. He shrugged off his coat and dropped it in a wet heap on the floor. He glared at the garment, knowing he should take out the mysterious packet and hide it somewhere safe. No one would come to his room tonight, however; he could leave it where it was until the morning.

Somehow he managed to remove his boots and wasn't surprised to find them full of sand and sea water. He stared at his bare feet. What had happened to his stockings? Without the weight of his coat and boots, he felt less tired and his head cleared. What was he thinking? Demelza had said she was unwell and he'd ignored this information. Without a second thought, he left his room and padded back to her apartment.

He knocked. On receiving no reply, he opened the door. He cursed under his breath. The girl wasn't asleep, but in a swoon. He dropped down beside her and felt for her pulse. Thank God! She wasn't in a deep coma; however, she might well succumb to congestion of the lungs if she remained all night in wet clothes.

He hesitated for a second, then did what needed to be done. Fortunately only her gown was damp; her chemise was dry enough to do her no harm. Tenderly, he placed her beneath the covers and stood gazing down at her. Even with the hideous bruise on her right temple, she was still the most beautiful woman he'd ever seen. His pulse quickened and he couldn't restrain himself. Carefully placing a hand on either side of her head, he gently kissed her lips. They were as sweet as he'd expected.

She was concussed; she might well cast up her accounts during the night. He daren't leave her unattended, in case she choked and her maid was busy elsewhere. He searched the dressing room for a suitable receptacle and placed it quietly by the bed. Then he pulled over the chaise-longue so he was within arm's reach of her.

He blew out most of the candles and returned with a coverlet he'd discovered in the parlour. Leaving one candle burning, he stretched out on the day bed and threw the patchwork quilt over his legs. His feet dangled over the end but he was too tired to care. He forced his eyes open to take a last look at his patient. She was pale but not unduly so. He would hear her if she stirred. He closed his eyes and dropped instantly to sleep.

* * *

Demelza jerked awake. Something had disturbed her. The candles had gone out. The storm had passed, and there wasn't even lightning to illuminate the darkness. She held her breath. There was someone in the room with her. Her pulse raced. Had one of the smugglers somehow found his way upstairs?

Her legs were unsteady, but she

would get out of bed and raise the alarm. She was silently pushing back the covers when a familiar voice spoke from close by.

'Remain where you are, Demelza. I'm too damn tired to pick you up from the floor.'

Outraged, she snatched the covers up to her chin. How dare he be in her bedchamber? He had ruined her good name. When Martha heard about his presence here, she would insist they get married at once.

The thought sent shivers up and down her spine. 'You should not be here, sir. You . . . ' She stopped and, despite her disquiet, her lips twitched. He was asleep. She could hear his rhythmic breathing. She sighed and settled back. Too late to worry about the consequences of his behaviour; she'd let him sleep. He was a brave man and deserved his rest.

Tomorrow he would find his life turned on end. Would it be so very bad to become Mrs Fairfield?

10

The sound of the curtains rattling roused Demelza from a deep, dreamless sleep. Betty's cheerful voice spoke from the window.

'Here we are, miss. Molly reckons you wouldn't want anything much this morning, not with your head being bad and all. Can you push yourself up a bit?'

'Of course. What time is it?' She risked a glance sideways, expecting to see the day-bed and signs of Lucas's recent occupation visible. To her astonishment, the item of furniture was where it always was, under the window. How could this be?

'Betty, where are my garments?' She expected her maid to tell her they were neatly folded on the clothes rack by the dressing room. This would prove Lucas had removed these items from her person and she hadn't imagined his presence in her room last night.

'Don't you be worrying about them, Miss Demelza. You dropped them on the floor and I've put them in the laundry bag. And it's after ten o'clock.' The girl placed the tray across Demelza's knees. 'Hot, buttered toast and tea. The doctor says as you're to stay in bed today.'

'How is Dr Fairfield this morning?'

'You wouldn't know he'd been saving sailors all night. Mrs Smith told me to take him his breakfast first thing and he was sleeping like a baby. Me and Josie took up water for his bath and he was downstairs eating a second breakfast in no time at all.'

'What about Captain Benbow and his crew?'

'Lawks, miss, you wouldn't believe it. Them sailors refused to come through the house; they rolled themselves up in the blankets and slept on the kitchen floor. Molly made them a right tasty breakfast and then they left. A diligence came from the village and took them off to Newquay.'

'I see. And the boys who were locked in the woodshed?'

'The doctor spoke to them and then they went along with the sailors.'

'Now I've eaten my breakfast, Betty, I wish you to help me get dressed. I shall sit in a chair by an open window in my parlour. I have no wish to remain in bed like an invalid.'

Twenty minutes later, she was comfortably seated and prepared to watch the world go by. She could hardly credit that the ferocious storm had departed and left a balmy summer's day behind. She had no wish to sew, and her head ached too much to allow her to read with any degree of comfort. Therefore, she would content herself with gazing from the window and waiting for visitors to alleviate the boredom. If she were honest, the only person she wished to see was Lucas. There were things she wanted to ask him, but she would have to be patient until he came to visit.

Good heavens, the grass was swarming with revenue men! No wonder Lucas had not had time to come and see her; he would be busy answering questions. She hoped Martha would keep the children away from the beach today; there could well be unpleasant sights not suitable for young eyes. The time flew by and she had no time to become irritated by Lucas's continued absence.

Betty reappeared an hour later with hot chocolate and freshly baked scones and jam. 'Here we are, miss. Thought you might be a bit peckish. Josie's taken the same up to the school room. Mrs Smith's keeping them busy this morning, but I reckon they'll be down to see you this afternoon.'

'Thank you, Betty. That looks quite delicious. Is Dr Fairfield still with the revenue men?'

'No, he's in the fields with Jethro. I reckon they're going to get them ploughed and planted. Them what's laying fallow at the moment.' She smiled and pointed to the activity on the cliff edge. 'Young Johnny and his gang won't be taking any chances in future. Bill says there's a new lot of revenue men come up from Plymouth. Things are going to be different around here from now on, you mark my words.'

When had her maid become so talkative? Demelza wasn't sure she liked this development, especially when she was on the receiving end of pertinent information that should have come to her directly.

'Thank you, Betty. You can leave this with me. I wish you to send Jimmy to the fields and tell Dr Fairfield I wish to speak to him urgently. This evening will not do.'

The children visited later on and were full of what they'd seen from the school room window, and they wished to be told as many gruesome details of the wreck and rescue as Demelza knew.

She felt decidedly flat after they departed with Martha for a brisk walk around the garden. Where was Lucas? Was he deliberately avoiding her? Until she saw him face-to-face, she couldn't be certain if she'd dreamt he was sleeping in her bedroom last night.

* * *

Lucas sagged against the hedge. He was more fatigued by his exploits last night than he'd realised. 'Jethro, I'll leave you to continue the inspection of the fields. I'm returning to the house.'

With luck and decent weather, Demelza's acreage could be ploughed and planted in time to get crops this autumn. Jethro had suggested buying a small herd of cows and opening the dairy again. The meadows were in good heart and more than able to feed half a dozen cows. The grass could be cut for winter feed if there was no further rain.

'Dr Fairfield, sir, Miss Demelza's asking to see you.' The stable boy wiped his face with his cap. Why had Jimmy felt it necessary to run out here? His lips curved. He knew exactly what Demelza wanted him for.

'I'm on my way back, lad. You take your time; it's too hot for rushing about.' He strolled into the kitchen and greeted Molly with a wave. 'I'm going to see Miss Tregorran. Is there anything you'd like me to take?'

'Bless you, sir, she only just had chocolate and scones.'

Lucas paused at the door. 'I'll not be dining here tonight, Molly.' For the next few days he intended to remain as far away from Demelza as he could. Until he found the courage to return to his ancestral home and put matters right there, he was in no position to make his feelings clear.

The poor girl must think herself demented. She would be trying to decide if she'd imagined his presence in her bedroom or whether he'd actually been there. She must not believe herself to have been compromised. When he eventually offered for her, it would be because he loved her and she loved him, and not through force of circumstances.

* * *

At last, Lucas was on his way. Demelza's hands were clammy, and waves of nausea threatened to make this meeting even more embarrassing. She dug her nails into her palms, hoping the pain would steady her. She would *not* cast up her accounts in front of him. He might be a doctor and well used to this sort of occurrence, but she wished him to see her in quite a different light.

The door to the dressing-room was ajar and her maid was in there with the mending. 'Betty, please let Dr Fairfield in and then leave the dressing-room door wide open.'

The girl scurried to do her bidding and curtsied politely as she opened the door for Lucas.

'How are you, my dear? You look

much better than you did when I left you hanging onto the door post last night.' He sauntered in, picked up a chair, and brought it over to the open window. 'Do you mind if I join you? There's a cooling breeze coming off the sea which makes sitting here less unpleasant.'

'Please do. My health has certainly improved; I wish I could say the same about you, Dr Fairfield. You look dreadful; I believe you've aged ten years overnight.'

His shout of laughter released the tension. 'How kind of you to say so, my dear.' He rocked back on his chair and stretched out his legs. 'I must own I do feel totally exhausted. I should never have ventured into the fields this morning, but remained resting in my room.'

'There's so much I want to ask you. Firstly . . . '

'No, my dear, your questions must wait. I want to know everything you can tell me about Reynolds. How long has he been squire? Have you met his wife at church?'

'What an extraordinary suggestion. Why should the squire and his wife attend our village church? It must be over five miles from their house, and they have their own church in the nearby village.'

His expression changed, no longer pleasant but deadly serious. 'He told me he would see us at church this Sunday. I got the impression he was a regular attendee.'

'Actually, now you come to mention it, Dr Fairfield, I don't believe I've ever spoken to him, and I've certainly never seen a wife. Why should they come here when they have Wadebridge so close, and that's a bustling market town?'

The chair legs dropped onto the floor with a crash. He leaned forward. 'How long has he lived in the neighbourhood?'

'The old squire died just before my father. If I remember rightly, Squire Reynolds arrived a month or so afterwards. As you can imagine, my own life was difficult and I had little time for anyone else.'

'I wish I'd been here to help you deal with matters. Such things should not have been left to someone as young as you.'

This would not do. He was claiming a familiarity that didn't exist. However much she yearned to be something more than a charity case, she couldn't allow him to believe he had any right to interfere with her life. 'You didn't know me then, sir. Indeed, we're scarcely more than strangers at the moment. We've only been acquainted a week or two, after all.'

'Exactly so! You're quite right to remind me, Miss Tregorran. I am merely your house-guest for a few weeks and will then be leaving to resume my responsibilities in Hampshire.' He sat back, his expression friendly and open, but she detected a certain wariness in his eyes.

'To return to the subject of Mr

Reynolds — do you suspect him of being in league with smugglers?' she asked.

'Far worse than that, my dear. I believe him to be in league with the French.'

Her mouth dropped open; she was rendered temporarily speechless. 'Good gracious! That hardly seems possible. Why should a French spy wish to live so far from Plymouth? Surely that's where he would discover secrets?'

'One might think so, indeed. However, one thing I am sure of — he's not the benevolent old gentleman he wishes everyone to think he is. He sent those two boys to discover the name of the ship that was wrecked. I can think of only one reason he should wish to have that information.'

'Which is?'

'He knew the *Rose of Newquay* was carrying more than illicit cargo. The fact that the looters appeared last night was coincidental. Those poor devils drowned when their boat capsized. If they'd known about the package, they would have attacked the captain and his crew.'

Demelza nodded. 'Of course they would have. A great shame the men lost their lives, but I have to admit I'm relieved they're no longer a problem in the village. I fear Young Johnny will have to find a new line of work.'

'I'm hoping your farm can offer them legal employment. You have several hundred acres scattered about the neighbourhood that could be brought back into full production.' He smiled in that particular way of his, and her irritation at his high-handed interference dissolved.

'Even with your generous contribution to household finances, I don't have the wherewithal to take on any more full-time workers.'

'I shall take care of their remuneration, my dear. No, don't poker up at me. Think of it as a temporary business loan. I shall record all my expenses in a ledger and then when you sell your

196

crops sometime in the future, you can reimburse me.'

Her spirits plummeted. He obviously had no intention of remaining at Tregorran. How would she manage when he left her at the end of the summer? She pushed the miserable thought aside. 'That's an excellent notion. The more men I employ, the better. But we have no work-horses here. Do you intend I should buy a team?'

'Not this year; I've made arrangements for a neighbouring farmer to hire his teams to you for as long as you need them. You're late getting land ready for sowing; his fields are done, and so his horses are presently standing idle.'

He pushed himself upright. He swayed and for an awful moment Demelza thought he would collapse. 'Dr Fairfield, you must go at once to your bed. We can discuss this further tomorrow when you're feeling better.'

'I shall take your advice, my love, and retire at once. If I fall asleep here I doubt anyone could carry me to my bed.'

She viewed his broad shoulders and nodded. 'I'm sure you're quite correct. One more thing, sir. What have you done with the documents Captain Benbow entrusted to you?'

'I've stowed them away safely. I thought about leaving today for Plymouth, but decided against it. I've told too many people I'm intending to depart on Monday, so thought it better I stick to my plan. Reynolds might well be looking for the papers and realise my reason for leaving early.'

'I'm honoured you've trusted me with your secret. I take it no one else knows about the papers?'

'No one. Remember, Miss Tregorran, you must remain where you are until I can examine your foot.' He straightened his shoulders and strode off without a backward glance. She wanted to throw something at his departing back. He was far too fond of issuing instructions. One might have thought he had been a real soldier, and not just an army physician, from the way he loved giving orders.

Martha and the children ate high tea with her, and by then she was more than ready to retire herself. The house was silent long before the usual time. No doubt everyone was suffering from a lack of sleep. The windows in her bedchamber were left open to allow the evening breeze to cool the room. She drowsed, listening to the owls calling and the seagulls returning to their roosts on the cliffs. She couldn't sleep. Her head was buzzing with the unpleasant thought that Squire Reynolds was a French spy and a miserable traitor. Could Lucas have got that wrong? The concept seemed quite bizarre.

Botheration! She needed the chamber pot. Carefully, she edged out of bed and half hopped her way across the room. The necessary receptacle was discreetly hidden in a cupboard. As she bent to recover it, she stilled. What was that?

The hair on the back of her neck stood up. Someone was on the terrace directly under her bedroom. She froze. There was a faint scraping sound, and then a recognisable click. Yes — that was one of the French doors being forced open.

11

Lucas prised open his eyes to see two small faces peering anxiously down at him. 'What's wrong, boys? Did something frighten you?'

Even in his sleep-befuddled state, he wondered why the children had come to him and not to Demelza or Mrs Smith. He heaved himself upright; he was able to see well enough, since he'd neglected to close either the curtains or the shutters when he'd fallen into bed that afternoon.

'There's someone downstairs. Tom wanted to use the pot and we heard the noise.'

Instantly wide awake, Lucas rolled out of bed. 'Boys, remain here. I'll go down and investigate.'

His pistols were still in the pockets of his riding coat. Would they be too damp to fire?

'Uncle Lucas, you've got your clothes on in bed.' Jack giggled and nudged his brother.

'And a good thing too — now I can investigate without wasting time.' He was about to remove his weapons when the door swung open. He pushed the children behind him and waited.

'Good evening, Fairfield. I see you've already got company. I would have preferred my visit here to remain a secret. Is there somewhere private we can converse?'

Reynolds had no gun in his hand. If it wasn't for his unconventional mode of entry, one would have thought it a social call. 'Tom, Jack, go and wake your sister. Tell her not to worry. There is no danger. However, you must all remain in her apartment until I give you permission to leave.'

The boys ran off to deliver their message, apparently unbothered by the unexpected visitor.

'Shall we talk in my parlour, sir?'

Lucas walked briskly across the bed-chamber, giving his unexpected visitor no option but to follow. He reached for the tinderbox.

'No, sir, we need no tell-tale light in here.'

The squire was a head shorter than Lucas, and twenty years his senior, but he was nevertheless a dangerous opponent. 'Well, sir, to what do I owe the pleasure of this nocturnal visit?'

'You have something that belongs to the government. I've come to collect it.'

'That's as may be, but before we discuss this matter I need an explanation.' In the gloom it was hard to see if the man had a weapon of any sort hidden beneath his coat-tails.

'My name is indeed Jonathan Reynolds, and I suppose by the nature of my residence that I am also the local magistrate and squire. However, first and foremost, I'm a government agent. We have been concerned for some time that either Tregorran or Trebetherick is being used not only for the passage of contraband, but also for something far more dangerous. Information is being smuggled out and in through one of these small harbours.'

'So that's why you've been turning a blind eye to the activities in the village. I thought it strange when Miss Tregorran told me.' Lucas was not ready to hand over the package. There was something else he needed to know first. 'What makes you think I could possibly have anything of value to the government?'

'Captain Benbow was a reluctant, but honest, courier. Word reached me that the ship on the rocks was very likely the vessel urgently awaited in Plymouth. I sent two employees to enquire but they failed to return.'

'I apologise for that, Reynolds. I thought *you* the traitor and the boys better away from your pernicious influence. Benbow said he would take care of them.'

'They'll do as well as cabin boys as working in my stables. Now, sir, am I to have the package? The information must be sent to London post-haste. I'm sure you understand . . . '

Suddenly the door leading to the passageway crashed open and a veritable termagant stood pointing a musket at the squire.

★ ★ ★

'Put your hands up or I will shoot you.' Demelza hoped she sounded convincing. Her legs were like blancmange and she was having difficulty holding the heavy weapon steady. She had needed the boys' help to carry the gun upstairs from the gun-room.

Lucas didn't look at all pleased to see her. In fact he looked furious.

'Miss Tregorran, what part of 'remain in your room' did you not understand? Give me that before you kill someone.'

'That man broke into my house. I came to rescue you.'

Lucas stepped forward purposefully.

She distinctly heard a snort of amusement from the intruder. What was going on here? She lowered the barrel.

'I shall speak to you later. I suggest you retire to your room and pretend nothing untoward happened tonight.' Lucas spoke quietly, as if to a recalcitrant child.

Incensed at his tone, she opened her fingers and dropped the musket on his stockinged feet. The result was everything she'd hoped. His expletives made her ears burn and she made a hasty exit, leaving him hopping and swearing in turn around his parlour.

She hobbled into Tom and Jack's room. The boys were hiding in their bed, quivering with excitement.

'Did you shoot him? We didn't hear a bang, did we, Tom?'

'Is Uncle Lucas all right?' Tom asked.

'You bloodthirsty boys! No, we misunderstood matters. Dr Fairfield was expecting this visitor. Unfortunately I dropped the gun on his toes. I don't think he was very pleased about it.'

'Now you both have an injured foot. What did this man want in the middle of the night?'

'I've no idea, Tom. No doubt we shall hear all about it in the morning.' If Lucas thought the twins could keep silent about such an exciting and unusual event, he knew nothing whatsoever about children. 'Now, settle down and go back to sleep. Thank you for being so brave.'

A sleepy voice called out as she was closing the door. 'I expect the man had come for the secret parcel. Goodnight, Melza.'

Good grief! How did he know about that? She was mulling this over in her parlour when the door opened softly. She swallowed the lump in her throat. She wasn't ready to face the formidable gentleman whose toes she might well have broken by her stupidity.

She could think of nothing sensible to say as he stood and glowered at her in the doorway. Eventually she unstuck her tongue. 'Has that man gone?'

'Yes. And he has taken the package. Reynolds is a government man, not a villain.'

She risked a glance at his feet. They appeared relatively undamaged. 'Well, that is a relief. It's so much better that a government agent break into my house in the middle of the night than a burglar.'

He pushed himself away from the door and walked without limping to within an arm's reach of her chair. 'What were you thinking? Not only did you risk your life by your foolishness, but you could also have set back your recovery by several days.'

This was too much for her fragile nerves. She gulped, sniffed, but couldn't prevent the tears from trickling down her cheeks.

'Sweetheart, please don't cry. Here, take this and dry your eyes.'

A damp handkerchief was thrust into her clenched fist and she mopped her face. However hard she tried, she couldn't stem the flow. Lucas muttered something under his breath and then she was lifted and replaced firmly on his lap. With a sigh of pleasure she snuggled into his embrace.

★ ★ ★

It took all his willpower not to tighten his hold and kiss her tears away. Instead he stroked her hair, loving the silky feeling beneath his fingers, and made soothing noises until her sobs turned into gentle, even breathing. She was fast asleep.

He sat with her cradled in his arms for a while longer. He would never forget the magnificent sight of his beloved girl coming to his rescue. There was no other young woman like her in the world. Not only was she beautiful, but intelligent and brave. He'd met his match. No other would do for him.

He eased himself from the chair. If he made sure he didn't put any weight on his damaged toes, he should be able to carry her into her bedchamber. He smiled wryly. He was making a habit of this, and if Mrs Smith were to hear of it they would have no choice about tying the knot.

He must stick to his plan of spending his leisure time in the village or the fields until he went to Plymouth in a few days. He would write to his lawyers as soon as he recovered their address from the rooms he'd taken at The Rising Sun. He would be in a better position to make decisions about their future when he'd heard from them. His responsibility was to his title and his lands — another detail he'd neglected to share with Demelza. Would she be willing to abandon her ancestral home and follow him to Hampshire?

He shuddered at the thought of his grandmother, the dowager Lady Maria Fairfield, knowing he was intending to marry a simple Cornish girl. He must have been mad coming here incognito — but having spent the past few years working as plain Dr Fairfield, using his unwanted title had not appealed to him.

He yawned, his jaw cracking loudly in the darkness. He was too fatigued to worry at the moment. Maybe after a good night's sleep he would see a clear path to a happy future.

12

The house was buzzing with talk of the 'burglar' and how brave both Demelza and the boys had been. She wanted to see Lucas and apologise for falling asleep in his arms, but he proved remarkably elusive. Serena bounced on the end of the chaise-longue later the following morning.

'Melza, it's ever so exciting. There's two teams of horses coming and they're going to be ploughing up some fields. We're going to watch and Mrs Smith says we have to count the time it takes for each furrow, and then we have to work out how long it will take to do the whole field.'

'What an interesting way to do arithmetic. Have you seen Dr Fairfield? Is he limping at all?'

'Uncle Lucas has gone somewhere to fetch something — I don't know what.

He's a bit lame but not as bad as you.' She tugged at Demelza's braid. 'Do you have to be up here much longer?'

'Hopefully I'll be back to normal in a day or two. My head hardly hurts now and I can almost walk on my foot. Now, run along. I can hear Mrs Smith calling you.'

★ ★ ★

She was pleased when the following day Martha agreed it was time to take up the reins of her life. 'I'm afraid Molly and Jethro are getting out of hand. The sooner you sort the matter out the better, my dear.' Martha tapped Demelza on the arm. 'I think we must appoint a housekeeper. Molly is not suited to this role — she's better confined to the kitchen.'

'I'm surprised Dr Fairfield hasn't done so,' Demelza replied tartly. 'I swear, that man has all but taken over this establishment.'

'He's not been in the house for more

than a few moments. Far too busy overseeing the men in the fields. That new gown looks quite lovely on you, my dear. Leaf green is a perfect complement to your eyes and black hair. Shall we go down? The children have the rest of the day to themselves. After all, it is Saturday today. They will come to no harm with Josie supervising them.'

Demelza needed no assistance to descend the stairs although her stiches were beginning to pull. 'Shall we take tea on the terrace, Martha?'

'I should like that. No point in ringing the bell; Betty's in the dairy and Molly will ignore it. I shall go and speak to her myself.'

Demelza picked up her book. A few minutes later Lucas appeared, dressed far more conventionally than the last time she'd seen him. She was pleased her hands didn't betray her disquiet.

'Miss Tregorran, I apologise for absenting myself, but I wished to get the repairs completed and the fields properly farmed.'

'You are so kind to have given up your time on our behalf. I have been wishing to apologise for dropping — '

'There's no need, my dear. I shall be leaving for Plymouth first thing tomorrow morning and your stitches must come out before I go. When will be convenient for me to do this?'

Why was he so formal? But at least he was easier to deal with when he wasn't teasing her, and she did want her stiches out. 'Right away. I'm eager to resume my normal activities. I have yet to discover a suitable puppy for the boys' name day next week. Do you wish me to go inside, or can you do what you must out here?'

'I shall attend you in the small sitting-room in five minutes.' He nodded, and with a brief smile strode off.

So he intended to remain aloof from Demelza in future. Her nonsensical imaginings had been put firmly in their place. She envied the easy relationship he'd developed with the children. If

215

there was to be no romantic involvement between them, she would have enjoyed being his friend at least.

Martha might return with the tea at any moment. Lucas must deal with the stiches upstairs. Ignoring the fact that he'd said he would be in the small parlour, she hobbled upstairs to her bedchamber and tipped water into the china basin. She didn't want him to handle her limb unless it was clean.

She was standing with her foot immersed in the water when he strolled in with his medical bag in one hand. His unexpected appearance caused water to slop over the rim and onto his boots. Mortified to be caught in such an indelicate position, and not sure how to remedy the situation, she froze.

'Allow me, sweetheart. Raise your foot and place it in the towel I'm holding.'

Keeping her eyes firmly averted, she did as he bid. He enveloped the wet foot in the cloth without touching her burning skin with his fingers. With professional calmness, he dried her and then placed a chair behind her. Her heart was pounding so loud she feared he would hear it. She dared not speak in case her voice betrayed her discomposure.

'This won't take a moment. I promise I shan't hurt you.' Cool hands gripped her foot and there was a slight tug as the sutures were removed. 'All done. If I'm allowed to say so myself, I did an excellent job. I doubt you'll even have a scar. Even the two ruptured sutures have healed cleanly.'

She looked down. Her eyes widened. Her foot looked so pale and slender resting in his strong brown hands. She snatched it back and shook out the folds of her skirt. 'Lovely. Thank you, Dr Fairfield. I've missed being able to walk along the beach.'

He straightened, shaking his head. 'I'm sorry, but you mustn't go down there for a day or so. The sand could get in and cause irritation.' He smiled, his eyes dancing with amusement.

'However, if you're prepared to wear your boots and stockings, then you may do whatever you wish.'

His light-hearted remark made her smile. 'Will you be dining with us tonight?' She particularly wished to know the answer, as her evening gown was now finished. He didn't answer for a moment and her spirits plummeted. He was going to refuse. Then he smiled and nodded.

'Yes. I gather from Molly we are to have *three* courses. Now she has a kitchen maid, she is determined to become more adventurous with her menus.'

Demelza frowned. 'I wasn't aware she discussed matters with you. I think everyone has forgotten I am mistress here.'

Instead of taking offence, he chuckled. 'Hardly that, sweetheart. I can promise you *I* have been well aware of your presence.' With that cryptic remark, he gathered up his belongings and left her to her jumbled thoughts.

Sometime later, she'd done all she

wished to. The children had shown her the improvements to the kitchen garden and the stable yard, which was more than enough walking for one day. 'I'm going to take Bessie and drive into Wadebridge. Would you like to come with me?' she asked them.

Jack and Tom were delighted. 'We haven't had a ride in a carriage before,' Tom said, dancing round her.

'It's not a carriage, silly; it's a cart,' Jack replied, pushing his brother. Before the squabble escalated, Demelza stepped in firmly.

'I think Mrs Smith might like to accompany us. Would one of you kindly find her and ask? We shall be leaving shortly. I've just to collect my bonnet and reticule and you three must tidy yourselves.'

★ ★ ★

The excursion was judged a success by the children. However, Martha developed a megrim and retired to her bedchamber with a soothing tisane. Josie, as usual, supervised nursery tea and put the children to bed.

'I shall come and read your bedtime story after dinner,' Demelza told the boys.

Several times as she sat at her dressing-table mirror attempting to arrange her hair, she was tempted to send word down to the kitchen that she too was indisposed. Despite her bravado of a few days ago, she was decidedly nervous about spending time alone with Lucas.

Eventually, she pushed in the final pin. It would have to do. Her new gown was draped over the end of her bed, ready for her to step into. She'd sewn a row of tiny buttons on the front so she could dress herself. The gown was in the new fashion, with the waist under her bosom. The flowing lines of the long skirt somehow made her seem taller. Keeping her back to the long glass until she was quite ready, she turned. The emerald silk swirled about her ankles, revealing the dainty evening slippers she'd gone especially to town to buy that very afternoon.

Good gracious, who was this beautiful stranger staring back at her? What a difference a lovely gown made. She was overdressed for a simple dinner, especially as Lucas didn't possess evening wear himself. But seeing herself so elegant, so sophisticated, gave her the confidence to glide downstairs to the drawing room where *he* was waiting for her.

★   ★   ★

The children had informed Lucas that Demelza's new gown was ready, so he'd made an extra effort himself. He hoped his royal blue, superfine topcoat and pearl-grey silk waistcoat would pass muster. He checked in the glass over the mantel that the snowy folds beneath his chin were satisfactory, and then glanced down at his boots. He nodded, pleased with their high gloss. They appeared none the worse for their immersion in salt water.

Light footsteps on the staircase warned him of Demelza's approach. He moved into the shadows so he could watch her descend. He'd done well this past week to keep away from her, when every time he heard her voice he'd wanted to take her in his arms.

Tonight was going to be difficult. His breath stopped in his throat. His fingers clenched the door frame. Descending the stairs was a beautiful young woman dressed in a stunning confection of green silk, her remarkable eyes sparkling like emeralds. She was *ravisante*, a diamond of the first water who would impress the highest members of the *ton*. Why had he thought her too unsophisticated to become part of his world? Even his demanding grandmother could not find fault with Demelza dressed as she was. She was every inch a lady — and would more than grace his family name.

Demelza paused by the open doors to steady her breathing, then stepped through. Lucas was there. He might not be in evening dress, but he looked magnificent. His eyes were dark and held that peculiar look she'd seen before. Heat spread from her toes to the crown of her head. He bowed formally and she dipped in a deep curtsy, praying she would not tip forward onto her nose.

He took her hand and raised her but didn't release her. He carried her fingers to his lips and kissed her knuckles. His eyes held her captive. She couldn't look away. Couldn't move. Her world stood still. For a moment there were only the two of them in it. Was he going to take her into his arms? What would she do if he kissed her?

A door banged and Josie bundled through. 'Dinner is served. Molly says as you're to come through or the crab soufflés will be spoiled.'

Lucas took Demelza's arm through his with a smile. 'Shall we dine, Miss Tregorran? I've taken the liberty of buying some French wine.' He winked. 'Surprisingly enough, there was an excellent selection to be had in the village.'

She relaxed. He preferred this teasing mood; she couldn't cope with his dark intensity.

'I believe one can purchase cognac and champagne as well.' Neither of them mentioned the word contraband; it would make the promised treat seem less enjoyable. Whenever Demelza heard talk of free traders in future, she would remember the horrible night when Lucas could have drowned.

'A glass of wine with one's meal is very acceptable, is it not? When my parents were alive a decanter of claret was always on the table at dinner time.'

The meal was delicious but Demelza scarcely noticed what she ate. She was completely engrossed by her companion. They talked of nothing very much at all; poked fun at politicians and laughed at the children's antics. They agreed that there was nothing worse than being obliged to attend an assembly or ball and to be crushed all evening with people they barely knew.

When the final cover was removed, Demelza was giddy with excitement, and she'd barely touched her glass of wine. 'Shall we stroll to the cliff, Dr Fairfield? It's so humid indoors. The latest storm appears to have passed us by this time.'

He was on his feet immediately, moving around to pull out her chair. She shivered as his warm hand brushed her bare arm. 'An excellent notion, but there's something I wish us to do first.' He paused behind her and she waited expectantly. Her heart thumped. What was he going to suggest? 'I wish to be given permission to use your given name and you must call me Lucas. I'm heartily sick of hearing myself addressed as Dr Fairfield.'

She was so relieved he hadn't suggested something improper that she agreed immediately to his unconventional suggestion. 'As the children already call you Uncle Lucas, I suppose *I* could do the same.'

His gurgle of laughter lightened the mood. 'Over my dead body, sweetheart. I might be a few years your senior, but I'm not old enough to consider myself your uncle.'

The terrace was pleasantly cool after the stifling heat of the dining room. Demelza viewed the black clouds racing across the sky. Perhaps she'd been wrong and a third storm was imminent after all. 'I think we'd better forego our constitutional, Lucas, unless you wish to be drenched. I certainly don't, as silk will not recover from such harsh treatment.'

Unaware he was standing close behind her, she stepped back into a solid wall of flesh. Heat burned through the thin material of her dress. Everywhere they touched, she was on fire.

His arms encircled her, holding h⸺ against him. His chin rested gently on the top of her head and she was almost sure he kissed it before stepping away. She didn't dare turn. Her bosom was heaving; it would be impossible to disguise how his embrace had affected her.

She took a deep breath and turned slowly. 'As we're not to take a stroll, shall we sit on the terrace for a while instead?'

He hesitated. 'Very well, Demelza. But remember, I'm leaving at dawn tomorrow so I cannot stay long.'

He made no move to escort her and she regretted her impulsive suggestion. 'So early? I hadn't realised. Pray retire at once, Dr Fairfield. I've no wish to detain you.'

He stiffened. 'Then I shall bid you goodnight, Demelza.' He nodded and stepped back into the house. He called out as he crossed the hall. 'Don't expect me back for a week at least.' And he was gone, leaving her to come in alone.

As she pulled the French doors closed behind her, forked lightning slashed across the sky. Thank goodness they hadn't remained outside. Rolls of thunder like giants kicking furniture rent the air. Putting her feelings to one side, she went upstairs to check on the children. Serena was wide awake and cowering under the bed covers. The church clock in the village had struck twelve before she was able to retire to her own bed.

When she rose the next morning, Lucas was gone. The house seemed strangely empty without him.

*   *   *

Life continued to improve for everyone at Tregorran House. Once the fields had been planted, there should be a surplus of food to help out families who were on short commons. Lucas wasn't expected for several days, but Demelza found herself constantly looking down the drive hoping to see him.

Two days after his departure, she went into the yard with the children to admire one of the teams of heavy horses borrowed from a neighbour. Demelza gripped Jack's arm. 'No, young man, you must remain at my side. These horses are here to plough our fields; they must not be petted.'

He relaxed. 'Can we watch again from the edge of the field? We like watching horses ploughing, don't we, Tom?'

His brother nodded and his hair fell over his eyes. 'We do, Melza. Can we go and see them working, please?'

'No, children. That would mean missing your lessons. I believe you've already seen them at their work.'

Martha wandered out from the house to join them. 'Good morning, Demelza. Children. What a fine sight a team of heavy horses is.'

'We want to watch the horses again, Mrs Smith, but Melza says we will miss our lessons,' Tom said.

'If you have no objection, Demelza, I

should be happy to take them to the field. We can use the experience to improve their mathematics as we did last time.'

'In which case, children, I shall leave you with Mrs Smith.' She turned to her sister, who was hanging back. 'Are you not going too, Serena?'

'No, Melza, I'm going to complete my composition. Mrs Smith said I can illustrate the pages when it's finished.'

Demelza followed her sister into the house. She paused in the hall. The sound of horses on the drive made her heart skip. She hurried to the door. Could it possibly be Lucas?

Of course it wasn't him. The pony and trap belonged to the vicar; their visitor was Martha's unpleasant sister-in-law. Mrs Barton was wearing a particularly ugly bonnet which suited her sour face. Anyone who could treat her dearest Martha badly was no friend of hers.

Demelza called up the stairs. 'Serena,

please find Mrs Smith before she disappears. Mrs Barton has come to call.'

★ ★ ★

Martha, Demelza and their uninvited guest were sitting on the terrace watching the children playing on the grass. Mrs Barton cleared her throat and fixed her beady eyes on Demelza. 'I'm not sure if you're aware, Miss Tregorran, but Dr Fairfield became embroiled in fisticuffs at The Green Man last week.'

'Thank you for bringing the matter to my attention, madam, but I can assure you he's very well behaved when at Tregorran House.'

The vicar's wife frowned. 'I don't think you quite understand, my dear. The fight was about *you.*'

Martha slopped her tea and looked angrily at her sister-in-law. 'That's quite enough, sister. Gossip is not something any of us should indulge in.'

Demelza interrupted. 'On the contrary, Mrs Barton, I wish to know exactly what happened.'

'Young Johnny asked if Dr Fairfield was courting you and your guest took exception to his comments and knocked him out.'

'I expect he was in his cups. Gentlemen behave quite badly when they've imbibed too much cider. I can assure you, Dr Fairfield and I are acquaintances only, and he will be leaving Cornwall at the end of the summer.'

The bringer of bad tidings departed soon afterward. Demelza went out to join the children in order to avoid being quizzed on the subject by her friend. She couldn't decide whether Lucas had reacted so violently because he disliked the notion of having his name linked with hers, or for some other reason she couldn't fathom.

She would speak to him in no uncertain terms as soon as he returned and insist that nothing so vulgar took place again if he wished to remain under her roof. At the moment she had an unblemished reputation in the neighbourhood, and wished to keep it that way. She half smiled. Imagine what would happen if word got out that Lucas had carried her in his arms several times and that she'd also sat on his lap. Heavens above! Then her good name would be in tatters for certain.

13

Only four days after Lucas's departure, the welcome sound of horses arriving in the yard brought Demelza to the upstairs window. She and Betty had been examining the bed linen to see what needed to be replaced and what could be mended.

Lucas was astride his massive bay gelding, which was staring down in horror at the children dancing round his feet. Waiting patiently behind him was a smaller, grey horse laden with saddlebags and parcels. Demelza spun and hurried into her chamber, glad her foot no longer troubled her. Satisfied she was tidy, she almost skipped downstairs and into the yard to greet him.

He dismounted stiffly, forced to grip the pommel for a moment. He must have ridden hard in order to return so quickly. She called as she ran across the cobbles, 'Welcome back, Dr Fairfield! We did not expect you for a further two days at least. You look exhausted; are you quite well?'

He grinned weakly. His face was sweat-streaked and his eyes dull with fatigue. 'I'm ashamed to admit I took a nasty tumble this morning. Perhaps I should not have continued my journey so soon.' He swayed dangerously and she leapt forward to press him back against his horse. The animal, sensing he was needed, stopped cavorting and remained stock-still to support his master.

'Come, lean on Jethro and me. We'll soon have you comfortable inside.'

Tom and Jack hovered, their faces crumpled. 'Is Uncle Lucas poorly, Melza?' Tom asked.

'Why has he got a lump on his forehead like the one you had, Melza?' Jack tugged on her sleeve.

'He fell off his horse, but I'm sure he's no more than dazed. Keep well away from Bruno; remember he doesn't like noisy boys.'

'Can we hold the grey horse, Melza? Jimmy's taking Bruno.'

The stable boy had already grasped the gelding's reins. She hesitated. This wasn't a good idea. The children could be in danger, especially from the massive horse. Where on earth was Bill? She was torn; Lucas needed her but the children's safety was paramount. 'Jethro, you and Betty take Dr Fairfield upstairs. I'll sort out the horses.'

Turning back, her eyes widened. Lucas's horse, who had previously looked ready to eat her brothers, had lowered his head and was gently nuzzling the boys. His ears were pricked as if listening to them chattering.

Jimmy grinned and scratched his head. 'Would you look at that, miss? Ain't as fierce as we thought. I reckon he's got used to us now and ain't so tetchy.'

Demelza walked over and patted the

huge animal's sweating neck. 'Bruno, I believe I could begin to like you. Come along, boys, let Jimmy take care of this one and we'll unload the grey.'

'Shall I take off the packages, Melza? If I stand on the mounting block I can easily undo them,' her sister asked.

'Thank you, Serena, but first take her to the water trough. Josie will be here in a minute or two to help us carry all these interesting parcels into the house.' Demelza forced herself to smile as if she wasn't concerned in any way about Lucas. 'Serena, I'll leave you and the boys to take care of the mare. I must finish the task I started before Dr Fairfield returned so unexpectedly.'

Molly was in the kitchen, preparing a tray for Lucas. 'The master says as you're not to worry, miss. I'm taking him up a nice meal. I reckon he'll be a lot better after that.'

Demelza stiffened. 'In which case, I'll start unpacking the belongings he brought back. No doubt I'll be given my next orders by *the master* when he's feeling more the thing.'

Molly scowled. She was unused to being spoken to so harshly. Immediately, Demelza regretted her comment. 'As I wish to speak to Dr Fairfield, I'll take up his meal. I think, after all the excitement, we could all do with a cool drink. Perhaps now is the time to use some of the lemons I bought the other day to make a delicious jug of lemonade?'

Jethro was on his way down when Demelza entered the hall. He nodded and beamed at her. 'The master's fair starving, my lovely. I hopes you got plenty on that tray.'

'Enough for several hungry men. The children are with the horses. I'd like you to bring in Dr Fairfield's baggage. By the way, where are Bill and Silas today?'

'They's ploughing, miss. Them horses don't drive themselves.'

Josie appeared from the rear of the house, her arms full of brown paper parcels. 'I'll leave these in the parlour, shall I, Miss Tregorran? I reckon the master will want to sort them out for his self tomorrow.'

Demelza closed her mouth with a snap, barely restraining the urge to forcibly correct the girl's comment. Were all the staff under the same misapprehension? This wouldn't do at all. In her house *she* should decide what happened. She should have explained things better to Molly and Jethro. She had neglected to put everyone straight on this matter. To the servants it must seem as if Lucas was in charge; he was certainly the *paymaster* after all. It scarcely seemed credible he had taken over so completely and in such a short time.

'Do that, Josie. Could you please make sure they're neatly placed and not higgledy-piggledy all over the floor?'

Fortunately, his chamber door was open and she was able to walk in without hindrance. The contents of the tray almost slithered off as she stared at the empty bed.

'Here, allow me to take that before you drop it. I'm famished. I don't want to lose a single morsel.'

She blinked and looked away, her cheeks turning pink. He was standing beside her in his breeches. The sight of his broad chest sent shivers down her spine. She'd seen him from a distance with as little on, but close up he was quite overwhelming. Shoving the tray into his outstretched hands, she turned and marched to the window seat where she sat, back firmly turned. 'Kindly put on some clothes, Lucas. A gentleman should not prance around his parlour in front of a lady the way you are.'

His hateful chuckle made her want to throw something at him. 'Very well, give me a moment and I'll find a clean shirt.' Drawers opened and fabric rustled next door, and then he spoke again. 'You can turn round, sweetheart. I'm respectable again.'

'And another thing. Kindly don't use endearments when addressing me. It's not at all proper and could be

240

misconstrued by anyone who over-heard.'

His eyebrows arched. 'I beg your pardon, my love. I address your siblings as affectionately and you don't object to that.'

'You know very well what I mean. Eat your meal. I have things I must discuss with you before we go down and join the children.' She half smiled; he was difficult to resist when he was in a teasing mood. 'I take it you don't intend to remain in bed? You have remarkable powers of recovery. Less than half an hour ago you were barely able to stand.'

He shrugged. 'Tell me what brings you to my apartment. It must be important.'

She told him of the unwanted visit from Mrs Barton and made it abundantly clear she disapproved both of his drinking and his fighting. 'I want your word that you will not further tarnish my good name.'

His lopsided grin slipped. 'Coming

here as you have is only going to add fuel to the rumours. For a girl who wishes to keep her reputation unsullied, you're going about it in a strange way.'

She looked at him in shock. He was perfectly correct; she must have been mad to come up here like this. A proper young lady would never enter a gentleman's apartment unless it was that of her husband. Hastily, she retreated toward the door. He held up his hand to stop her.

'Please, don't go. The damage is already done. I think your staff are loyal; they'll not go into the village and gossip about either of us. I have things I must tell you.'

He looked so serious, her heart all but stopped. 'Have you decided to leave us again?'

He didn't answer — his mouth was too full of meat pasty — but his eyes sparkled with humour. He swallowed and took a long draught of cider. 'That, my love, remains to be seen. No, don't poker up . . . I was jesting.' He munched his way through half his meal before speaking again. 'This gossip. I know how we can silence the tabbies. What happened is something I've given serious consideration to. We can say we are betrothed.'

Her mouth dropped open. How could he say such a thing so casually? Was this another jest? Unsure how to respond, she busied herself refilling his pewter tankard.

'Demelza, my love, I should not have blurted it out like that. I have feelings for you and I thought that you returned them. Am I incorrect?'

Hardly daring to believe that he had made a genuine offer, she raised her head. His eyes blazed into hers.

'We have known each other such a short time. It's far too soon to talk of . . . to talk of such things.'

Slowly, he replaced his cutlery and pushed his chair back. She was pinned to her seat by his gaze. Her heart pounded and she was finding it hard to breathe. Dramatically, he dropped to one knee and clasped her trembling hands.

'My angel, I love you. From the moment I saw you on the beach I knew you were the one I've been waiting for. Will you do me the honour of becoming my wife?'

She wanted to say yes, to throw herself into his arms and declare her love, but somehow she managed to hold back. 'I think I do love you, Lucas, but I can't say yes. You have obligations on the other side of the country and I have them here.' She twisted her hands in her lap. 'It's far too soon to talk about such things. When we know each other better, please ask me again.'

For answer he stood and pulled her close to him. His arms encircled her waist and his mouth closed over hers. She should protest, but a heady excitement spiralled through her and she stretched to return his kiss. Eventually he released her and her legs threatened to give way. He smiled down, his eyes tender.

'Darling girl, if you love me then you will not hesitate to come with me when I leave. But I shall respect your wishes and not insist on an answer until you've had time to consider.'

'Thank you. Now, I shall sit over there on the window seat whilst you finish your repast and tell me all about your trip.'

He returned to the table and resumed eating. Between mouthfuls he looked over. 'I'm a determined man, sweetheart. I've never been denied. I shall convince you that *your* life is with me in Hampshire.'

Demelza blinked back her tears. She loved him so much, but how could she ever agree to marry him when his plans didn't include Serena, Jack or Tom? At no time had he mentioned them; the offer was for her alone. She would not marry a man, however much she loved him, if he didn't love her darlings as much as she did.

Lucas finished his meal. 'It's good to be home again. I believe Molly's as good a cook as any I've met abroad.' He brushed off the crumbs and pushed the tray to one side.

'Another thing, Lucas. I wish there to be no further intimacies between us. I'm certain Serena is beginning to suspect our feelings might be engaged. I no longer wish us to spend time alone.'

He slammed his hand down and the tray all but leapt from the table. 'God's teeth!'

Demelza shot up from the window seat. She wished he wouldn't use bad language or bang the furniture in this way; it was most disturbing. 'You might have been an officer, but please keep your military language to yourself. I take it you don't agree with my suggestion?'

'I certainly do not. I have told you I love you and want to marry you. I know you will say yes when you've thought about it for a while. I don't want to hear anything else.'

Tears spilled down her cheeks. Why couldn't he understand her hesitation?

Did he think her a heartless sister? She straightened and faced him. 'Then I will give you my answer. No, I cannot marry you. Now, excuse me, I have . . . '

Suddenly he was beside her, too close . . . her pulse raced. She couldn't think straight. His arms slid around her. She trembled. She opened her mouth to protest but her words were smothered as his lips closed over hers in a tender kiss. She pressed her hands against his chest but he ignored her feeble protest.

This felt so right. She relaxed into his embrace and her body was suffused with a delicious sensation she didn't recognize. Then sanity returned and she shoved him violently. 'Stop this at once. You can't take liberties like this. I told you. I am *not* going to marry you.'

His arms dropped away and she was free. 'I beg your pardon, sweetheart. I should not have done that but I couldn't bear to see you so distressed.'

'Enough; I don't wish to discuss it.

Are you a man who keeps your word?'

A flash of anger crossed his face. 'I am a gentleman. When I give my word, I keep it.'

'In which case, sir, give me your word that you'll not attempt to kiss me again.'

She held her breath. For a moment she thought he would refuse. Then he nodded curtly and turned away to pull on his jacket.

'Good. Also I want no further mention of there being feelings between us.'

He glanced toward the window and grinned. 'Very well, whatever you say. Excellent, my purchases are coming in. Fetch the children. I have something to give each of you.'

With a resigned sigh, she went into the yard to find Serena and her brothers. They were hanging over the fence, feeding the new arrivals with bits of stale bread cadged from Molly.

'Serena, Jack, Tom, you must come in now. Uncle Lucas wants to speak to you.'

The three of them scampered across the cobbles. Jack arrived first at her side. 'That big horse is funny. He picked Tom up by his collar.'

'Good heavens, I hope he didn't hurt your brother. Were you teasing him, Tom?'

'I wasn't, Melza. Uncle Lucas's horse is my friend now. We were playing. Look, he's laughing and nodding at us.'

Demelza glanced across and indeed, the massive gelding looked as if he was doing just that. His long, yellow teeth were bared and his head was bobbing up and down. 'It's wonderful to have horses here again. Two weeks ago we had none, and now we have three.'

'More than that, Melza. We have the farm horses too.'

'And we have lots of people to help us. There's Jimmy and Bill in the stables. I like it with Uncle Lucas and Mrs Smith living here. I never want them to go away.'

'Uncle Lucas has his own home to go to at the end of the summer, Serena, so we must make the most of him whilst he's here.'

The last of the packages had been transferred to the drawing room. The children bounced with excitement at the sight of so many interesting objects. Lucas was examining each in turn.

'Ah . . . at last. I was beginning to think nobody wanted a gift from Plymouth.' He tossed a brown paper parcel to each child and winked at Demelza.

'Mrs Smith, this is for you. I thought the new novel everyone is talking about would suit you.'

Martha exclaimed when she unwrapped the book. 'Look, my dear! *Pride and Prejudice*. I've heard so much about it. Thank you, Dr Fairfield.' She rushed off with her prize, presumably to begin reading it straight away.

'I've got a pretty shawl. Look, Melza, it's got daisies and primroses embroidered all over.' Serena rushed across and threw herself into Lucas's lap. For a second his arms remained at his sides, and then he hugged her back. 'Thank you, thank you, Uncle Lucas. It's exactly what I wanted.'

Tom and Jack were having difficulty with their string but refused offers of assistance. 'We can do it, can't we Jack? We're not babies.' Eventually the knots were undone and the paper ripped away to reveal half a dozen lead soldiers for each child. Their screams of excitement at being given such treasure brought tears to Demelza's eyes. How could he be so kind to her siblings and not wish them to be part of his life? Was it guilt that prompted him?

'Remember your manners, boys. What do you say to Uncle Lucas for such a wonderful gift?'

They, too, flung themselves at him, shouting their thanks; he laughed and ruffled their hair. 'I'm glad you like the soldiers. Now off you go and play with them. You're far too noisy to be inside.'

'Melza, I'm going to help Molly make scones for tea. Can I wear my wrap this afternoon, or does it have to be kept for best?' Serena asked.

'I should keep it for Sundays, sweetheart. But as long as you don't wear it whilst you're getting covered in flour, you may keep it on for the rest of today.' Her sister ran out, leaving Demelza alone with Lucas. She smiled. 'Thank you for the children's gifts. I can't imagine how you managed to purchase such ideal presents.'

'Aren't you going to ask me what *your* gift is? Which parcels do you think contain something for you?' With dancing eyes, he tossed three into her lap. 'I had to guess your size. I hope you like them.' Without waiting for her to thank him or open the packages, he headed for the door. 'The grey mare is also yours. Her name's Silver. I couldn't resist her; she's perfect for you. I take it you can ride?'

She clutched her presents to her chest and her throat clogged; she could only nod. He smiled a toe-curling smile and sauntered off, leaving her surrounded by other unopened parcels. He had given her a riding horse. This was the best gift in the world.

She frowned at the parcels he'd left behind. No doubt these items were his and he expected her to transfer them to his closet. He was obviously accustomed to having servants running after him. It would be churlish to complain when he'd been so generous.

Scooping up as many of the items as she could, she carried them upstairs and dumped them on the chaise-longue in his sitting-room. Botheration! She shook her head. Now her things were muddled up with his and she could hardly open everything in order to discover which were meant for her. It was unseemly for her to handle his garments. Betty could do that when she'd finished her other morning tasks.

What she *would* do was check that her breeches and riding boots still fitted. She smiled ruefully when she put them on. The breeches would need a belt of some sort to keep them up. She was shocked to think how much weight she must have lost for them to fall straight down as they did. Her boots were equally loose, but with two pairs of stockings inside they would do. She'd never had a riding habit. Around here women rode astride like their men folk. Her lips twitched at the thought of Lucas's face when he saw her dressed like this.

14

Demelza changed back into her every-day clothes. Her first ride must wait until the mare had recovered from her arduous journey. She wasn't sure where Lucas was, but had no wish to come face-to-face with him at the moment. She decided to walk into the village when she'd finished sorting the linen, and gauge for herself the amount of gossip associated with her name.

With her bonnet swinging from one hand and her reticule in the other, she stepped out onto the terrace. Oh dear, another storm was imminent. She couldn't recall another summer when the weather had been so turbulent.

'So, here you are. You have been conspicuous by your absence, my dear. Are you by any chance avoiding me?' Lucas was sitting on the stone bench, legs stretched out in front of him, apparently unmoved by their emotional interlude upstairs. However, his complexion was a trifle pale and the lump on his forehead was turning an interesting shade of blue.

'I'm not. I've been completing a task upstairs.'

He smiled. 'I've got my evening rig. Shall we all dress for dinner?'

'You don't look at all well, Lucas. Perhaps you should dine in your room tonight?' She raised a hand to forestall his protest. 'And anyway, I've nothing suitable. My silk is too hot for such a humid evening.'

'I've brought you another gift, definitely something less formal. Will you wear it for me tonight?'

She was tempted to refuse. For him to purchase garments for a lady not his wife was quite unconventional. However, if he'd been kind enough to think of her when he was away, the least she could do was wear his gift. 'I will. I was intending to walk into the village but I think another storm is brewing so will remain in the grounds instead.'

'Good. Then I shall take your advice and take a nap in my room. I should hate to fall asleep at the table.'

He left her on the terrace and was halfway up the stairs when she recalled *her* gifts were still on his day-bed. If she was to appear in whatever he'd bought her, she must go at once and collect the items. Perhaps one of the staff had already done this; she'd check first.

However, when she enquired, Betty shook her head. 'No, miss, I'm sorry but I've not been upstairs. Shall I go now?'

'No, thank you. Dr Fairfield has gone to his chambers.'

Tom and Jack ran past, clutching their soldiers. 'We're going to build a fort outside, Melza, come and see.'

'Sorry, Jack. I have duties to attend to. Perhaps I can come later on.' The boys rushed away, too excited by their gift to be bothered by her refusal. The children loved Lucas; they were going to be devastated when he vanished from their lives.

Her love for him was of a different sort. He occupied her every waking minute. She was beginning to wonder if his arrival was going to turn out to be more of a curse than a blessing to her family.

His parlour door was firmly closed. Surely he couldn't be asleep so soon? He'd only gone up a few minutes ahead of her. She knocked loudly but received no reply. She lifted the latch and peered round the door. He was sprawled on the day-bed in his shirt sleeves and breeches, apparently sound asleep. No doubt he'd learned to snatch whatever rest he could whilst on the Peninsula and had the knack of dropping off immediately.

The parcels were in a heap on the boards and there was no way of telling which three held her items. They were all topsy-turvy, one on top of the other. On hands and knees she carefully prodded and poked and peeped, but discovered nothing feminine inside the brown paper. There were crisp shirts, cravats, two waistcoats, undergarments, breeches, and a smart bottle-green jacket.

Disgusted, she sat back on her heels and looked around for the missing packages. They were nowhere in sight. Of course, he must have taken them into *her* room. What a goose she was not to have checked there first. She tiptoed out, closing the door quietly behind her.

But her gifts were not there either. Mystified, she crept back. Only then did she spot a mound of brown paper on the far side of him, to the left of his stockinged feet. She'd wasted a good half an hour scrabbling about on the floor. Edging around him, she leant forward to collect the first item. To her consternation his arm shot out and captured her wrist. His eyes opened and he smiled lazily. 'I was waiting for you to collect these, my love. If you had thought to ask, I would have told you they were beside me.'

Thoroughly flustered, she tried to tug her hand free. His grip tightened and before she could steady herself, he jerked and she tumbled headlong into his arms. This was not supposed to happen. He'd promised he would not kiss her again.

'You gave me your word . . . '

'If you recall, sweetheart, you asked me to promise not to kiss you, but you will remember I carefully refrained from answering. A nod of a head is not a promise.' His hands soothed her as if she were a fretting child; his gentle strokes somehow chased away her reservations. 'Look at me, my darling. I want to see your lovely eyes. I could drown in their depths. I am under your spell; you have enchanted me like a wild Cornish wood nymph.'

Then his lips touched hers and she was lost to all common sense. All that mattered was she loved him and he loved her. Somehow they would find a way to make a future for themselves and she would persuade him to take on the children as well. She would tell him she had changed her mind and would become engaged to him after all.

He drew back after kissing her and gently moved her. 'Go, I must rest. There are things we need to speak about this evening.' He rolled over and within seconds was genuinely asleep, his deep even breathing filling the silent room and allowing her no chance to reply.

Gathering up her presents, she returned to the privacy of her own domain. With shaking fingers she tore off the paper. Her eyes widened as she held up the gown. The garment was an unusual shade of greenish-blue, not a shade she'd ever seen before, but quite similar to the colour of a duck's egg.

The gown was in the new fashion and would suit her slender figure and rounded curves to perfection. The neckline was heart-shaped and delicately sewn with the palest turquoise beads; these were repeated around the edges of the little cap sleeves and on the hem. She held the dress up in front of her and spun around the room. The gown was going to fit perfectly, elegant enough to wear in the evening but ideal for the dining room at Tregorran House. With a sigh, she draped it over a chair back.

He had kissed her, said he loved her and wanted to marry her. So why did she still hesitate? She had behaved appallingly. A well-brought-up young lady should not have responded to his embrace the way she had. Mama must be turning in her grave. She would have told her there was no choice but to accept the offer. Demelza must move to Hampshire even if it meant leaving the children behind.

Tears spilled down her cheeks and she brushed them aside. Lucas was a good, kind man. Eventually he must agree to allow her siblings to join them. Why couldn't he stay here instead? She shook her head; she already knew the answer to that.

Lucas was strong, determined; he would not let something as trivial as a romance stand in the way of his duty. If he believed his life was elsewhere, restoring his ancestral home, then that was what he would do.

She must decide. Should she do what was right, or what was in her heart? Did her good name mean more than her brothers and sister?

No, she had promised Mama she would take care of them. She couldn't break her word, even though it would break her heart to let him go. Therefore, she must make the most of every precious second that remained. At least then she would have memories to keep her warm in the dark winters that would follow his departure. She was glad now she hadn't had time to tell him of her change of heart. This secret she would keep from him and the rest of her family.

* * *

Demelza was certain she'd never looked better. Her new gown fell in gossamer folds about her ankles. When she was stationary her toes were hidden, which was a shame as her gifts had included matching slippers. Somehow her neck appeared longer, her eyes larger; and instead of her arms looking thin, tonight they seemed elegant.

Grand ladies of society would be shocked rigid by the fact her skin was not white but golden brown from the hours she spent outside in the sunshine. Her mouth curved. Lucas's face was darker than her own, but then anyone attached to the military spent most of their time outdoors.

He'd gone downstairs some time ago and was moving about restlessly on the terrace below her window. Where was Martha? She must go and see what was keeping her friend. It would be wise to remain chaperoned this evening.

Demelza knocked quietly. Receiving no response, she pushed open the door to discover the bedchamber in darkness and the shutters drawn. 'Martha, are you unwell again?'

The huddled shape on the bed moved slightly. 'I am a martyr to sick headaches, my dear. I'm afraid you must go down alone tonight.'

Having made sure there was nothing she could do, Demelza quietly closed the door behind her. How odd that these headaches appeared at such inopportune moments. Could fate be conspiring to push her and Lucas together regardless of her reservations?

She had no option. She was already tardy, so must go unaccompanied.

The children had gone to the beach with Josie. She couldn't delay her descent by visiting the school room. Taking a deep breath, she straightened her shoulders and walked toward the stairs. Her pulse quickened. What was he going to say to her? Was he thinking of their future? Had he realised why she had refused him and changed his mind about the children?

Footsteps on the flagstones warned

her Lucas had come in. She stiffened, hardly daring to move and see his expression when he saw her in her finery. Demelza slowly turned, being careful to keep her ankles decorously hidden beneath her skirts. Her eyes widened. Who was this handsome gentleman smiling down at her so charmingly?

In his evening garments, he was devastating. She forgot about her own appearance — she couldn't take her eyes from his.

'Move along, miss,' Molly said. 'These here plates won't take themselves to the table. Betty has your first course in her hands.'

Blushing furiously, Demelza apologised to Molly and rushed past Lucas into the dining room. Not waiting for him to pull out her chair, she sat down and busied herself unfolding the napkin so she didn't have to look at him when he entered.

'The gown is perfect on you, Demelza. And I feel a different man entirely in these smart togs — small wonder you were surprised at my appearance.' He grinned at Betty, who had followed with the second tray. 'This looks and smells delicious. Thank you.'

They sat in silence until the room was empty. Demelza was reluctant to reach out in case he took her hand.

'This is ridiculous, sweetheart. The prawns in cream are getting cold; the sole and bass fillets will not improve by being left to congeal. Are you going to sit like a statue?'

She stared at him frostily. 'I believe it's usual for a gentleman to help a lady, not the other way around. I'm neither your wife nor your daughter, so I have no obligation to wait on you.'

His expression darkened. For a moment she wished she'd not spoken, then he smiled politely and began to dish up the food. She ate just enough so Molly wouldn't be offended. The atmosphere in the room was decidedly chilly. Somehow she got through the meal, but had never been more grateful when the dessert was removed and she could leave.

'You still have half a decanter of claret to finish, sir, so I'll leave you to it.' Hardly the graceful words of the perfect hostess, but she needed to get away from him. He'd done nothing to actually offend her, but his offhand behaviour had hurt.

* * *

Lucas watched her go. He had behaved shamefully, treating her as if she was of no account. Twice he'd taken advantage of her innocence and put her in an impossible position. She was gently born and would know a gentleman didn't kiss a lady unless they were betrothed. There was only one thing that would put matters right, but he was reluctant to push her into an engagement that was for some strange reason apparently not to her liking.

Something was holding her back. The only thing he could think of was that she had no wish to leave her beloved Cornwall. He could offer the little ones so much more than they could get in this remote part of the world. His eyes lit up as he imagined leading Serena onto the dance floor at her come-out ball. She would be as beautiful as her sister and make a brilliant match. He would employ the best tutors for the boys and they could attend his own school when they were older.

He was used to getting his own way; his powers of persuasion were legendary. He would not be defeated in this battle. He would win her over somehow. He was sure she felt the same as he did; she wouldn't have allowed him to kiss her otherwise. It didn't make sense. He was a wealthy man and perfectly presentable. Why wasn't she delighted to be receiving an offer from him?

Tarnation! Had she somehow discovered he wasn't plain Dr Fairfield, but Lord Lucas James Fairfield, peer of the realm? Did the thought of becoming a member of the aristocracy appal her? After all, she wasn't used to living formally and spending her days doing nothing more active than embroidery.

He snorted. He had no time for such flummery — so why should he expect his darling girl to conform? If Grandmother didn't approve, then so be it. He would speak to Demelza tomorrow and reassure her she had nothing to worry about. She would make a perfect Lady Fairfield.

*   *   *

The grass was damp, and impulsively Demelza took off her slippers to feel the dew beneath her feet. It was a lovely summer's evening. Nothing must spoil her mood of optimism. Tonight she would remind herself that Lucas's generosity had changed the family's fortune and not dwell on what might have been.

She had yet to discover a puppy for the boys. There had been nothing suitable in the village. Tomorrow she would ride Silver around the neighbourhood until she found an animal she liked.

The sound of childish laughter coming from the cliff path drew her across the grass. As the children emerged from between the gorse bushes, Lucas called her from the house. She ignored him. The little ones would think it strange if he didn't come over and see what they'd collected. He had discarded his smart jacket and tossed his cravat aside. He looked much more familiar in his shirt sleeves and breeches.

'See, Melza, Jack and I have got mussels, and Serena's got crabs and shrimps,' Tom said.

She turned to examine the children's treasures and then Josie arrived, red-faced and breathless.

Serena tugged at Demelza's skirt. 'Melza, why doesn't Uncle Lucas come to see? Did you have an argument?'

Lucas wasn't walking toward them;

he was standing ramrod-straight on the terrace, waiting for them to approach. She ignored Serena's question.

'I 'spect he's tired, isn't he Jack?' Tom said.

'He's got new boots on, Melza. Can I have some too?'

'One day, Jack, I'm sure you can.' They had almost reached the house. Why didn't Lucas move? Her cheeks flushed. The boys rushed forward as if nothing was the matter and eagerly showed him the contents of their buckets. Immediately he was the old Lucas and dropped down on his haunches to exclaim at every shell and crab.

Josie took her new duties as nursery maid seriously. 'I think it's time for you all to go up; it'll be dark soon.'

'I'll be along later to read you a story. You may play with your soldiers for half an hour if you go to bed without a fuss,' Demelza told them.

Serena hung back. 'Do I have to go to bed at the same time as them? I'm nearly grown up. I think I should be allowed to stay up longer.'

Demelza was about to agree when Lucas stepped in. 'Not tonight, Serena. You have been given an instruction; kindly do as you're told.' Without another word, she vanished.

Did he think he was their guardian? How could he presume to interfere when he didn't even want them in his life when he left here?

'My sister's behaviour is none of your concern, Dr Fairfield. If you wish to remain here, kindly remember your place. You are my paying guest, not the master, and it's high time you understood your position.' She raked him with an icy stare. 'My life is here with the children, protecting our inheritance. Tregorrans have lived here for hundreds of years. *I* am mistress of this establishment and you would do well to remember it.' She stalked off. Her nails bit into her palms as she blinked away her tears. Had her words convinced him she held him in dislike? If he tried to persuade her to accept him, she would succumb.

She didn't care that she might have damaged her good name. What had happened had not been his fault. He had made her an offer. She had decided not to accept. The ruination of her reputation was entirely her concern. She would never marry, so what did it matter what another gentleman might think?

If she couldn't be the wife of the man she loved, she would remain a spinster forever.

★   ★   ★

Lucas wanted to call her back but thought better of it. She'd made her feelings perfectly clear. He could hardly force her to marry him because he had overstepped the mark. He strode back to the dining room and slumped at the table. He drained his glass and refilled it, slopping the wine over the brim. A dark red stain spread across the polished surface. He swirled his finger in the spill and sighed.

However much he loved her — and he was quite sure she was the one for him — if she wouldn't leave here, he must accept that. Anyway, a gentleman ought to put his duty first. He couldn't abandon his responsibilities and remove himself to the wilds of Cornwall in order to be at her side.

A wife should follow her husband. That was how things were done in society. Unless she was prepared to move, he could see no future for them. He would leave the next morning. He could not share a house with the woman he loved and not be able to speak of it. Too dispirited to think further, he trudged upstairs and dropped onto his bed fully clothed.

15

Demelza heard Lucas leave at dawn. How could he creep away without saying goodbye to her and the children? How was she going to explain his disappearance? How could she tell them it was her fault he had gone and that he didn't want *them* in his life?

She wasn't going to tell the children the truth. Far better to prevaricate for the moment, and let them become accustomed to his absence, before revealing the true state of affairs. It would be easier to speak to them whilst they were in the school room, as they would be too busy to ask awkward questions. Her feet dragged. The nursery stairs seemed steep this morning. She pushed open the school room door to find Martha drawing a map on the blackboard whilst the children worked industriously at their slates.

'I'm sorry to interrupt your studies but I have some important news to give you.' She felt a tingle of embarrassment trickle down her spine. 'Uncle Lucas has had to return to Plymouth to complete his business. He made a special journey yesterday in order to bring us our gifts. Wasn't that kind of him?'

'Will he be back for our birthday, Melza?' Jack asked.

Martha came to her rescue before she was embroiled in more falsehoods. 'I'm sure Dr Fairfield will come if he can. Your sister has given you the news; kindly return to your studies.'

Smiling her thanks, Demelza slipped away. This improbable explanation would not do for anyone but the children. When she had come to terms with the loss of the man she loved, she would explain everything to Martha.

★   ★   ★

She moped about the house for several days, and even the lure of the beach was not enough to raise her spirits. Martha respected her privacy and made no comment about her unlikely explanation for Lucas's departure. Eventually Demelza decided she must explain the whole to her family, and she invited them to join her in the drawing-room.

'I have to tell you that Dr Fairfield will not be returning. Unfortunately, he has had to return to his estates in Hampshire earlier than expected. This is a great shock to all of us and he will be sorely missed.'

Serena scrambled to her feet, her face white. 'You lied to us, Melza. It's your fault he's gone. He would have stayed if you'd been nicer to him.'

The boys joined their sister by the door. Tom clutched Serena's hand. 'We don't like you anymore, Melza. You've made Uncle Lucas break his promise and you've told us lies.'

Before she could stop them, they vanished through the French doors. She gathered up her skirts and ran after them, but they dodged around the house and disappeared. She hurried to the stables, their favourite place. 'Jimmy, have you seen the children?'

The stable boy looked up and scratched his head. 'No, miss, don't reckon I have. Ain't they in the school room?'

'No, they have run off. Please let me know at once if they come here.'

He touched his cap and she continued her search, but in vain. She looked everywhere, but despite her constant calling they didn't respond. Where could they be? She even went down to the beach, but to no avail. Eventually she returned to the house to be greeted by Martha.

'Let them be, my dear. They will come around. Children are resilient; they won't bear a grudge, I promise you.' Martha patted Demelza's hand. '*I* shall go after them in a while. It's hardly surprising they are upset at your news. Indeed, I find myself equally perturbed. I didn't take to the young man at first, but thought him here to stay. I believe that . . . ' Martha dabbed her eyes. 'Indeed, my dear, I actually encouraged the romance between you.'

'I beg you, Martha, please don't talk about it. What's done is done. I must learn to live without him. I believe you were going to the vicarage this afternoon. I must find the children and put matters right and you must attend your meeting as planned.'

'At least you have sufficient funds to complete the improvements. So however sad you are at the moment, my dear girl, you must not regret his coming.'

Martha was correct. Demelza would never be sorry she'd met Lucas. He had brought laughter back into the house and given her Martha; she would not repine on what she had lost, but remind herself of what they had all gained.

The staff must know the news, but they seemed less upset than the children, which was puzzling. She had expected her mood of despondency to be reflected by everyone else. She was waylaid by Jethro and Molly as she hurried through the kitchen for the second time.

'Miss Tregorran, we's wanting to talk to you after supper, Jethro and me. If that be all right.'

Puzzled, Demelza paused. 'Of course. But not before matters have been put right with the children.'

Jethro nodded and sucked his empty clay pipe. 'Don't you fret, my lovely, them three will come to no harm.'

'I do hope you're right.'

She was too distressed to enquire why they wished to speak to her later. She must put it all behind her and move forward for the sake of the children. However, images of Lucas constantly filled her head. What was he doing now? Was he striding about his vast estates without a care in the world? No, he was not so shallow — he still had his family's untimely deaths to think about. That was enough trouble for any man. She prayed he would find happiness one day and be able to look back on his short time in Cornwall with pleasure.

The children were still avoiding her. They came in briefly to snatch a bite at mid-day but ran off again immediately. Supper time would come soon; hopefully they would be hungry and come in. She would walk to the beach and give them time to eat before she went in for her meal. Martha was waiting in the house.

She didn't have the energy to scramble down the path, so she sat at the top, gazing out to sea. The water was calm; it was hard to believe a ship had foundered on the rocks so recently. A slight scuffle behind her made her jump. She looked around but saw nothing. Then the gorse bushes parted and a row of little faces peered through.

'We've come to fetch you back for supper,' Serena said as she held back the prickly branches to let her brothers through. 'We're all sorry for being horrid to you. We know you miss Uncle

Lucas even more than we do. Mrs Smith told us.'

Tears trickled down Demelza's cheeks as she hugged them to her. 'And I'm sorry too.'

'Can we have a puppy for our name day next week?' Tom nudged his brother and they both smiled hopefully.

'I suppose I shall have to tell you: I've already selected one. Shall we go in the trap and collect him tomorrow morning?'

Her suggestion was greeted with shrieks of excitement. Only Serena looked serious. 'A puppy isn't the same as having Uncle Lucas here with us.'

'I know, sweetheart, but it will help us come to terms with losing him.' She kissed her sister and stood up. Hand-in-hand, they strolled back to the house. Demelza thanked God that at least matters were put right within her own family. She supposed she would never leave Tregorran House. When the boys married and wished to bring home their brides, there would be ample accommodation for all of them. She would be both aunt and substitute grandmother to any children they produced. She brushed away unwanted tears at the thought that she would never have children of her own.

The supper table was subdued. The boys were exhausted after having been outside all day, and Serena was thoughtful. In future meals would be taken informally; even Martha was happy to eat in the kitchen with the children. The dining room held too many memories for them all.

Hot water had been heated in the copper and the boys took a bath in front of the kitchen range. Serena settled for a jug of hot water for her ablutions.

'Here, I'll take that for you, Serena. You go on up, my lovely; your sister be wanting a quiet sit down,' Josie suggested.

Tonight Demelza tucked the boys into bed. 'Mrs Smith will be along directly to tell you a story. I must go down; Molly and Jethro wish to speak to me.'

She hesitated outside the kitchen. Jethro was in the yard, checking the journeymen had completed their tasks satisfactorily, but she could hear him stomping back across the cobbles. The idea of farming all the acreage must be put aside, for without the money Lucas had promised his plans were no longer possible. This must be what Jethro wished to talk about.

Demelza was drained. Too much had happened in the past few days, and she wasn't eager to talk about the situation again. She straightened her shoulders and marched in.

Molly was standing by the open back door but turned as Demelza entered.

'What is it you wished to say to me, Molly?'

Jethro limped in and doffed his cap. 'It's like this, Miss Tregorran. Jethro and me want to say a word or two, if you'll let us.'

'Please, Molly, you must speak freely.'

Demelza hid her smile. The housekeeper and her husband seldom did anything else.

Chairs scraped as they sat. Jethro cleared his throat, but said nothing. Molly spoke for both of them. 'It's like this, miss. We're happy here and don't want to leave. But what we want to know is, what will happen to us when your young man comes back? He'll want to marry you but he'll not want to stop here, not a gent like him.'

Demelza stared from one to the other, unable to form a coherent sentence. 'I don't think you fully understand. Dr Fairfield won't be returning. He has duties elsewhere.'

She expected them to look shocked, to sympathise, but they didn't. Jethro broke the silence. 'He'll be back, never you fret, my lovely. He'll soon realise where his true *duties* are. So, will you be a-going with him when he comes?'

'Please understand: Dr Fairfield and I have agreed we do not suit. He must marry a young lady from a different background. I must get on with my life here and forget about him; you must do the same.'

This conversation was most inappropriate, but there was no stopping Molly. 'I reckon you do yourself down, miss. When you was dressed up in your fancy clothes you weren't no different than them ladies in grand houses. That young man of yours is head-over-ears in love with you. He'll not be able to stay away; you mark my words, he'll be back.'

'How kind of you to say so, Molly. But this is where I belong, where generations of Tregorrans have lived. The estate is my brothers' heritage and I must stay here and manage matters for them.'

Jethro shoved back his chair. 'I don't reckon places is as important as people, miss. I'm a-going outside to smoke me pipe.'

Demelza left the kitchen more confused than ever. They were correct; Lucas did love her and she loved him.

Circumstances had conspired against them; their separation was nobody's fault.

Martha joined her in the drawing room and the remainder of the evening passed in talking of the future. Together they would make a life for themselves. With Martha's financial input, the annuity, and the money Lucas had left, they would be able to live comfortably. With luck, the estate would soon be self-supporting once more.

Demelza went to bed happier than she'd been earlier in the day. The children were sleeping soundly and the house was quiet. She examined her hands in the candlelight; they were less red and work-roughened than they had been a few weeks ago. She must complete her sewing and continue to update all their wardrobes.

If one day Lucas returned, he would find them changed. Her desire to become more ladylike was for him. Perhaps when he saw the children well-dressed, not raking about in faded clothes up to their knees in mud, he might reconsider his decision and include them in his offer.

Jethro was right. She could trace her ancestry back hundreds of years. Tregorrans had always lived in this neighbourhood. Although she might not be as grand as families who lived in the Home Counties, she could hold her head up proudly in any drawing-room if she had to. The children loved Lucas and she had believed he reciprocated their feelings.

Why didn't he want them in his life?

★ ★ ★

The next day, she was completing a list of tasks for Josie and Betty when her attention was attracted by two small faces pressed against the window. She smiled. 'I'm sorry, Molly. I'll have to finish this later. Get the girls to start on the first items. There's plenty to keep them busy for today.'

Collecting her bonnet and reticule,

she hurried around to the stable yard. Bessie was already between the shafts and the children were bouncing up and down on the seat, waiting for her. There was no sign of Martha.

'Is Mrs Smith not coming with us?'

'No, she's going down to the village to collect a parcel,' Tom said, nudging his brother.

'Is she fetching us a gift, Melza?'

'It's rude to ask such things, Jack. You must wait until Saturday.' Serena caught Demelza's eye and her lips curved in a secret smile.

Obviously her sister was involved in whatever Martha was fetching. 'I'm sorry I'm tardy. Do you have something in which to put the dog? I vividly recall Patch having no control over his bodily functions for the first month or two.'

Her comment sent the children into fits of giggles and she scrambled up, laughing with them. After untying the reins, she clicked her tongue and the trap rolled forward, bumping noisily over the cobbles until it reached the drive.

The return journey was enlivened by the little bundle of black and white fur doing his best to jump out of the vehicle. 'Children, you must hold that scrap more securely. Poor Bessie is becoming quite agitated by the rocking and bouncing.'

'Scrap — that's what we'll call him,' Serena said, clutching the wriggling puppy to her chest. 'Scrap, settle down, Melza's getting cross with you.'

The puppy licked Serena's hand, wagged his tail and fell fast asleep. 'At last. I've never known so much energy in something so small. Whatever you do, boys, don't wake Scrap up again,' Demelza reminded them.

'He's made a puddle on the floor, Melza,' Jack said gleefully.

'Never mind; it will soon dry in the sunshine. But remember, you three have promised faithfully to clear up his little mistakes if they occur indoors.'

Tregorran House glowed in the

afternoon sunshine; the grey slates shone and the leaded windows sparkled. She tried to be happy, to enjoy the moment, but found it hard.

Serena handed the sleeping dog to her brothers to take care of. 'You said that *I* could drive once we were home; can I do it now?'

'Yes, I shall get down here and walk. You can take Bessie round to the stables. Bill and Jimmy will be waiting to take care of her. I shan't be long; I just need a little time to myself.'

She watched the old mare walk amiably toward the yard. In fact, the animal would have gone without any guidance, but Serena was enjoying the feel of the ribbons in her hands. What they needed to raise their spirits was a party. There hadn't been a celebration of any sort since her mother had been taken ill, and that was just after the boys were born. She would tell her friends and neighbours and have a garden party. There would be jugglers for the children and dancing for the adults.

Her steps quickened and by the time she reached the house she was running. 'Martha, are you back? We have a party to organise and only two days to do it.'

'I hesitated to suggest it, but I thought exactly the same thing myself. We cannot afford anything lavish, but we can invite some of the local children so the boys can play games.'

'No, I want to include everyone. We used to do this at harvest time. Folk from the village all bring a contribution, so the expense will be negligible.'

When she put the idea to her staff they were enthusiastic. By teatime everything was planned and Jethro went down to the village to spread the word. There was no need to send out invitations. Anyone who wished to could attend the event. Demelza was relieved to hear that Tregorran was once more a friendly place now the incomers had gone.

Scrap seemed content to curl up in his wooden box in the corner of the scullery, and the children skipped off to bed as if Lucas hadn't gone. Demelza wished she could shrug his departure off so easily. Whilst she had been busy writing lists and issuing instructions, she'd scarcely had time to dwell on her sadness. But now, alone in the darkness, her tears fell freely. Her pillow was sodden before she eventually fell asleep.

★ ★ ★

Bruno was reluctant to leave Tregorran. The gelding hung his head and refused to do more than a lumbering canter, and Lucas hadn't the heart to use his whip to urge him faster. In this fashion they meandered onward, overnighting at disreputable roadside inns where Lucas was convinced he'd picked up crawlers. On reaching Plymouth he took rooms at the hostelry he'd stayed at previously. He must arrange for the business loans he had promised Demelza to be paid to her. In his haste to leave, he'd quite forgotten this essential matter.

The landlord greeted him with unexpected enthusiasm. 'Mr Fairfield, a letter has arrived this morning by express; and as you didn't leave your direction, I didn't know what to do with it. I'm right glad I can hand it over.' The portly innkeeper passed over an impressive package liberally dotted with sealing wax. Lucas frowned. What now? Had some other disaster overtaken the estate? Not wishing to peruse the contents under the curious eyes of the landlord, he strode outside and found himself a quiet corner before breaking the seals. He scanned the contents with growing disbelief. How could this be?

He'd always thought his brother a prudent man; that he held the family estates as a sacred trust for future generations of Fairfields. How could he have invested so poorly? Lucas read the letter a second time. He shook his head. Everything was gone — the estates, the farms — all gambled away on dubious investments. God's teeth!

This changed everything. He didn't have to return to Hampshire; he could go back to Tregorran. Although he would have to tell Demelza about his title, there was no need to adopt it if he was living informally in Cornwall. His grandmother would be annoyed that he wasn't returning, but she had her own life with her society cronies and would hardly notice his absence.

He clutched the letter to his chest and looked skywards. The Almighty had answered his prayers. He hadn't wanted to occupy his brother's shoes, and now he didn't have to. His personal fortune was more than adequate to support a wife and family. Surely Demelza wouldn't refuse him, now she didn't have to leave her beloved home?

Lucas returned to the inn and told the landlord he would be leaving first thing. Bruno needed to rest or he wouldn't be fit to ride in the morning. He must write to his lawyers immediately. He would get the missive on a mail coach when he went to look for a jeweller. He intended to purchase a betrothal ring before returning.

★ ★ ★

Saturday dawned bright and clear and Demelza got up eagerly for the first time since Lucas had abandoned her. The boys had received new outfits from her, two storybooks from Martha, and a paint box and paper from Serena. Scrap was still their favourite present. The puppy, despite his frequent unpleasant mishaps, was already loved by everyone.

The party was planned for mid-day. High tide came in early evening and the men would need to take out their fishing boats. A makeshift band of musicians would play lively jigs, and there would be a fire-eater and stilt-walker. Also, there would be bobbing for apples, pin the tail on the donkey, and various other treats for the children.

Every guest had brought a contribution to the feast and soon the wooden tables were laden with good food. Demelza had supplied several barrels of cider and small beer, and there was lemonade for the children. By the time the food and drink were consumed, the final game played and the guests departed, the sun was slowly sinking below the cliffs.

'Well, boys, did you enjoy your anniversary?'

'We did, but Uncle Lucas promised he would be here. I thought grownups always kept their word.'

'I'm sure he would have liked to be here. Now you must come inside and wash your hands and faces. I think you can forego your story tonight. There's been more than enough excitement for one day.'

Even Serena didn't protest at being sent to bed early. The children were exhausted when Josie took them up. The day had been successful and Demelza had almost managed to forget her sadness.

'Why don't you go down to the

beach, my dear?' Martha suggested. 'The fresh air and solitude will do you good. I shall sit on the terrace and read my book. Josie is upstairs and will take care of the boys if they need anything.'

'I will, thank you. I've not been down since Lucas left, but this evening I think I would enjoy a walk.' She stared down at her dainty slippers. 'I shall change my footwear first. I should really change my gown as well. Sitting on the sand will not improve this new muslin.'

'I fear it's already mired with sticky fingers; a little sand can hardly make matters worse. I'm sure Betty will remove the damage when she launders your dress tomorrow. Run along and change your shoes. The light will soon be gone and that cliff path is too steep to be climbing then.' Martha smiled. 'Don't forget to take something to sit on, my dear. The sand will be wet.'

16

The tide had turned and already there was a strip of yellow sand running along the base of the cliff. The blood-red streaks trailing across the water as the sun set made the vista even more picturesque. Demelza's eyes filled. Lucas should be here to paint the scene. He'd shown her some of his work and although he professed to be an amateur, his paintings were beautiful. He'd captured the light and colour of Cornwall in a way she'd never seen before.

This evening she would sit on the beach and allow herself a few moments to recall what might have been. She settled herself comfortably on the sack, her back against the warm cliff face, and allowed the gentle rhythm of the waves to soothe her. Her eyes flickered shut and she dozed.

Something jerked her awake. What

was it? She was about to scramble to her feet and investigate when a finger appeared in front of her.

'You stay right where you are, girlie. You ain't going nowhere. You owes me for what your man did.'

She recoiled. The smell from this creature made her gag. She didn't have to ask who he was; she recognised him as one of the nasty incomers. Lucas had said they'd all drowned, but this one must have somehow swum ashore and was here to take his revenge. The wretch must have been hiding down here, scavenging what he could from the sea, since the night of the disaster.

'Dr Fairfield no longer resides at Tregorran House. I can give you enough to allow you to escape the revenue men.' She started to stand up but he lurched towards her and punched her down.

'Ain't that a shame, then? You ain't going nowhere. You stop right 'ere until 'e comes to fetch you. And if 'e don't — ' He gestured with a filthy finger towards the outgoing tide. ' — it'll be a big tide in the mornin'. No sand to sit on then.'

'My men will come down to find me very soon and they will be armed — '

'They ain't comin'. It'll be full dark soon. They would've come by now.'

Her fingers clenched — he was right. She must pray that sometime during the night she found the opportunity to escape, or they would both drown in the morning.

* * *

Lucas vaulted from the saddle, calling for Jimmy or Bill to come and take his exhausted gelding. Devil take it! Where the hell were they?

'Come along, old fellow. I'll sort you out myself.'

Twenty minutes later he strode into the kitchen. That, too, was empty. He shouted as he reached the hall. 'Demelza? Mrs Smith? Anyone?'

There was the patter of feet from

outside. The back door burst open and Josie appeared. 'Oh, sir, such an upset! Miss Tregorran has not come back from the beach and everybody, apart from myself and Mrs Smith, has gone to the village.'

'How long has Miss Tregorran been gone?'

'Since I put the children to bed.'

He ground his teeth. 'When was that? An hour? Two?'

'I don't rightly know, sir. It was still light and now it's full dark. I reckon it must be two hours.'

Lucas ran to the terrace. Where was Mrs Smith? A flickering lantern was moving toward him. He hurried to meet her.

'Oh, Dr Fairfield, I cannot tell you how pleased I am to see you. I've called over the cliff but Demelza doesn't answer. I daren't descend that path in the dark. It's too steep for me.'

'I'll go down at once. I'm sure she's perfectly well, madam. I expect she's fallen asleep on the sand.' He frowned.

'It's unfortunate the entire staff are absent. I'll need a blanket, Josie; please fetch me one.'

The maid vanished. Mrs Smith looked apologetic. 'Indeed it is, Dr Fairfield. I gave them permission to go once the debris from the party had been cleared away.' The redoubtable lady was looking at him strangely. 'Dr Fairfield, we didn't expect to see you here again.'

'I know. I asked Demelza to marry me but she refused. She said she couldn't leave Tregorran. I couldn't remain here under those circumstances. I love her, Mrs Smith, and have returned to try again.'

'My dear boy, I was sure you felt the same as Demelza. She has been so miserable these past few days. I'm at a loss to know why she should have refused your offer. But you're here now and you can ask her again.'

'My circumstances have changed, madam.' The French doors flew open and the children emerged.

'Uncle Lucas, Uncle Lucas, you've come back! We knew you would. You promised to be here for our name day.' Jack flung himself forward and Tom followed. Even Serena joined her brothers.

He knelt and hugged them. 'Children, I've missed you. I'm here to persuade your sister to marry me. But first I must fetch her from the beach.'

Josie arrived with a blanket. 'My word, what are you all doing down here, and in your nightshirts too?'

Serena answered. 'We heard Uncle Lucas and just had to come down. He's going to marry Demelza.'

'Enough, young lady,' Mrs Smith admonished. 'If you wish to remain out here you must behave yourself.'

Lucas threw the rug over his shoulder and set off on the double. He didn't take the lantern, as this would make his descent more difficult.

★   ★   ★

The noise of falling stones alerted Demelza. Someone was descending the path. Before she could call out a warning, her captor grabbed her from behind and put a stinking hand across her mouth.

Bill, or one of the other men, must be coming at last to see why she was lingering on the beach. She attempted to wrench the smuggler's hand away, but he was too strong for her and tightened his grip across her throat, making it difficult to breathe.

Her eyes widened and tears brimmed over. How could Lucas be here? Even in the gloom she recognized his massive outline. No one else had his height or breadth of shoulders.

Lucas stopped. His voice boomed in the darkness. 'Release Miss Tregorran if you wish to live.'

'I ain't bothered. You killed me friends — now I'm going to kill your lady.'

The arm across her neck tightened — her head was spinning — Lucas would be too late to save her.

With a roar of fury, Lucas surged forward and she was free. Whilst she recovered her breath, she heard the sound of blows and then the thud of a falling body.

She couldn't speak. She was shaking from head to toe.

'My darling girl, come here to me. It's over. I have you safe.' He gathered her close and she entangled her fingers in his hair. His lips claimed hers and she was lost in a wave of love.

Eventually he raised his head and cradled her face in his hand. 'Sweetheart, are you injured?'

'No. My throat is sore, but otherwise I'm unhurt.'

His teeth flashed white. 'Thank God I did return. Mrs Smith is beside herself because she gave your men leave to go to the village; no doubt they will return too inebriated to be of any use. If I hadn't come back — '

She snuggled close. 'Please don't think about that. You're here and you rescued me.' She pulled back and stared at him. 'Why are you here? I thought you gone for good.'

'I couldn't stay away. I love you. Somehow I'll convince you to marry me. I cannot live without you at my side.'

Her euphoria at his unexpected return vanished. 'Lucas, it matters not that you love *me* if you don't want Serena and the boys . . . '

His arms tightened and he scowled. 'Devil take it, what nonsense is this? Why should you think such a thing of me?' He shook her none too gently. 'I'm tempted to toss you in the sea for your stupidity.'

She tugged his collar and stared at him in horror. 'But you never mentioned them when you asked me to marry you — '

'Of course I didn't. I assumed you would know they were included without me having to mention them specifically. What a pea goose you are, my darling. I can't believe you've put us both through this misery over such a misunderstanding.'

How could she have got this so wrong? She could think of only one way to answer his quite justifiable complaint. She pulled his head down until their lips met in a kiss that told him everything. She forgot the horror of the past few hours, forgot everything, and just gave herself to the moment. He smiled down at her.

'I've so much to tell you, but this is not the place. First I want to know if you've changed your mind. Will you marry me, my love?'

'I will. As long as the children are included, I don't care if we have to leave Cornwall. I want to be at your side; that's more important than remaining here.' She stroked his bristle-covered cheek. 'However, my love, I should like to receive another formal offer from you. Am I not to get one?'

He laughed out loud. 'I can hardly go down on one knee at the moment, but I shall do so with all ceremony as soon as we're home safely.' He glanced behind her and this reminded her of the man he'd felled.

'What about that man, Lucas? Did you kill him?'

'No, he's merely stunned. He'll recover his senses and crawl away before the morning. I fear his mind has gone. His actions were those of a madman.'

'They were — he intended us both to drown.' She shuddered and moved nearer to Lucas, relaxing in his embrace. From now on, nothing could hurt her or her family.

'Come along, my darling girl. We have to negotiate the path. Are you able to do so after your experience?'

'If you climb behind me, I'll be safe. I told you, I'm unharmed.'

When they emerged on the grass, there were lights in the windows of Tregorran House and three small figures were standing on the terrace with Martha.

'Good heavens. I left the children fast asleep. What are they doing up?'

Lucas dropped a kiss on the end of her nose. 'They came down when they heard my voice. Mrs Smith gave them permission to remain. Also, I wish to give Tom and Jack the full set of soldiers I've purchased for their name day. These will complete their army.' He squeezed her hand. 'I think it better if we don't mention what just took place. Tell them you fell asleep.'

'Of course — I shall explain to Martha later. I'm glad they are up. I want those I love the best to share in my happiness.' She paused and touched his lips. 'My darling, I do hope Martha is included in your plans? I couldn't bear to be without her now.'

He stopped abruptly. 'I suppose I'm to take your cook and handyman as well?' He sounded fierce but she knew he was joking.

'And a leaking puppy who answers to the name of Scrap. I fear your well-ordered life will be upturned when

I become your wife.' Forgetting they were being observed from the terrace, she stretched out and kissed him tenderly. 'I love you, Lucas. I knew from the moment I saw you on the beach that you were going to change my life.'

The sounds of cheering and applause echoed through the night. When eventually Lucas raised his head, Demelza could scarcely speak for joy. She would worry about what was to become of Tregorran House tomorrow. Tonight she would enjoy her happiness.

The children could hardly contain their excitement. Lucas raised his hand and they fell silent. 'Quiet, all of you. I shall answer everything in a while. But first we must both have a hot drink and something to eat.'

Josie rushed off to fetch what was wanted, and Lucas led Demelza to the drawing-room and guided her tenderly to the sofa. 'However, there's one thing I must do first.'

He dropped to one knee, taking her

hands in his. His eyes glittered. He was as moved as she. 'My darling girl, will you do me the honour of becoming my bride?'

'I will. I love you, Lucas, and will do everything I can to make you happy.'

Tenderly, he slipped an emerald ring over her knuckle. 'I hope you like this. It reminded me of your lovely eyes.'

'It's beautiful, Lucas. Thank you.'

Before she could say anything further, he sprang to his feet and gestured to Martha and the children. 'Now, I have exciting news for you all. I received a letter from my lawyers informing me that my brother had made unwise investments and lost his inheritance. The estates don't belong to me, but the bank. Even if I wished to restore the house, I couldn't afford to do so. It's going to take me years to redeem the mortgage.' He beamed at Demelza. 'I hope you don't mind if we remain in Cornwall once we're married.'

'You have always acted as if you were

the master here, so things will continue as before,' Demelza replied. His smile sent waves of excitement swirling around her body.

'*Touché*, sweetheart. I see we are going to deal famously together.'

Then Serena spoke up, her expression anxious. 'Does that mean, Uncle Lucas, that you have lost all *your* money as well?'

Martha immediately took the child to task. 'Serena, don't be impertinent.'

'No, Mrs Smith, Serena has said what you must all be wondering. I had no wish to inherit my brother's wealth. To be rich beyond my wildest dreams because he and his family had perished, stuck in my craw. I'm not fabulously wealthy, but have more than enough to restore this magnificent house to its former glory and take care of all of you.'

Demelza caught his hand in hers and pulled him closer. 'I don't care how much money you have. As long as you're here at my side I shall be the happiest girl in Cornwall.'

Eventually the children returned to their beds, Martha retired to hers, and Demelza and Lucas were alone. She had been becoming increasingly concerned as the minutes passed that there was something worrying him. Something he couldn't speak about in front of the children and Martha.

'Lucas, what is it you haven't told me? There must be no secrets between us.'

He clasped her hands in his and stared earnestly at her. 'I have not been entirely truthful, my love. I've been masquerading all summer. I'm not plain Mr or Dr Fairfield but Lord Fairfield. You will become Lady Fairfield on our marriage and if we are blessed with a son, then he will inherit my title.'

'Good heavens! A lord? You don't look like an aristocrat, my darling, but you do have a lordly and overbearing manner.'

'You don't mind that I deceived you?'

'Of course not. I doubt anyone would have believed you anyway. We're simple folk around here and we believe that a real lord must live in a grand house and only travels with a valet and a carriage-load of baggage.' She smiled. 'Do we have to use your title?'

His fingers tightened around hers. His voice was gruff. 'Not if you don't want to, my love. One day we might have to return to Hampshire — but until then we shall live as plain Dr and Mrs Fairfield, at Tregorran.'

'I don't care where we live as long as we are all together.'

He raised her hands to his lips and gently pressed a kiss on her knuckles. 'You have my solemn oath, sweetheart, that from this day forward we shall never be apart again.'

THE END

VET IN DEMAND

Carol Wood

For Elissa Hart, the shock of her father's sudden death is bad enough. To find his veterinary practice in such a poor state, both financially and with dated equipment, is just as upsetting. The only way to save the practice is to take on a partner able to make a real investment — and Adam Kennedy is willing to do just that. Can Elissa reconcile her resentment of Adam and his bold ideas with her growing attraction to him?

THE SHAPE OF SUMMER

Barbara Cust

When Anna Blakeney is offered the temporary job of looking after the Chatham children, Sara and Jeremy, her guilty feelings about the deaths of their parents in the car which Anna's father was driving make it impossible for her to refuse. She instantly dislikes the children's half-brother and guardian, Drewe, but while he is away she reckons she can sort out her problems with her boyfriend Ricky. Then Ricky meets someone new, and Anna is surprised to find that her own passions have changed in the most unpredictable way . . .

ESCAPE FROM THE PAST

Iris Weigh

Driving northward in the hope of leaving behind her old life and painful memories, Clare Bowers takes a wrong turn in the mist and ends up in a ditch, from which she is rescued and taken to stay at Moorlands Farm. The owners have had their own tragedies in the past, and there is still a bitter feud between them and the Laytons at the nearby farm. Then Clare meets the darkly handsome Richard Layton, and her past threatens to overtake her again . . .

TAKE A CHANCE

Sheila Holroyd

When Tessa unexpectedly loses her job, she tries to console herself by impulsively going on holiday to Spain, hoping that a sun-soaked restful break will help her face the future. But instead she finds herself involved in the affairs of Tom, an Englishman who has settled in the country, and two children who have apparently been abandoned by their father. She does her best to help them all, but will Tom's past stop her from finding happiness?

THE HOLLY BOUGH

Pamela Kavanagh

When Catrin and her family are taken on as farm help, word soon spreads that she has 'a winning way with livestock, and a rare touch with plant and herb cures'. But Catrin's burning desire is to find the person who abandoned her as a baby on a pile of straw in a stable one Christmas. It is an obsession that even puts at risk the future she might have with the local smith, Luke . . .